Lots Of Love

Patsy Collins

Contents

1. Nice Enough..1
2. Perfection In Everything...5
3. Quiet..11
4. Waving Goodbye...16
5. Losing Battle..22
6. Eyes Down, Look In..28
7. Catching The 5.37...32
8. Thirty Years On..36
9. What Use Is A Hen That Doesn't Lay?........................43
10. Tender Touch...47
11. The Gift Of Understanding.......................................51
12. It's Just Not Fair...57
13. Listen To Me..63
14. Looks Familiar..68
15. A Changed Woman...73
16. For The Love Of Fennel...77
17. All Talk..82
18. Diamond Disaster...88
19. Just Two Months..92
20. Trying To Be Nice..100
21. Life's Little Sacrifices..105
22. Finishing The Sequence..113
23. Hopeless Romantic...117
24. A Bag For Life...122
25. Love Will Wait...126

1. Nice Enough

"… delighted your daughter accepted," Hari said.

Beside him my little girl glowed. Other than matching happy expressions, they looked so different. He's far taller, broader, darker; a brooding mountain of a man. Elizabeth's eyes sparkled brighter than the tiny chips of diamond in her ring.

Reminding myself she wasn't still thirteen and this was her decision to make, I smiled and said, "Congratulations."

My husband Simon saved the situation with his enthusiasm. He hugged them both, then fetched glasses and champagne.

My hugs were less than Simon's. I didn't miss a word out there, they were less everything. I'm much smaller, so my hugs were too. Following after his, naturally mine were less spontaneous and, as he was already offering glasses overflowing with froth, they had to be quicker.

I wiped up the tiny amount of spillage, so no one would slip on the kitchen lino.

Simon, Hari and Elizabeth chattered excitedly. No one mentioned a date, so I asked.

"We were thinking of July, but we want to check that's convenient for everyone," Hari said.

"I think it is for us, isn't it, Simon?"

"Any day you pick will be fine for us."

"Of course it will," I said. Simon was right, we weren't the kind of people who have lots of important events booked up and in any case our daughter's wedding would come first.

"Have you told your parents?" I asked Hari.

"Not officially, though I think they've guessed. We're driving up there this evening and staying overnight."

That led to talk of cars, and Simon offered to check the pressure in the tyres on Hari's vehicle. Likes his gadgets Simon does. The electric pump is his latest toy. It wasn't just that. Obviously he cares about the safety of Elizabeth and our future son-in-law. Probably too, he wanted to give me a moment with Elizabeth.

"Let's have a proper look at that ring," I said as soon as they boys headed for the garage.

It was really pretty. An amethyst, her birth stone, in the centre with tiny diamonds around it like flower petals. They sparkled in the sunlight streaming through the kitchen window.

"It's lovely!" I said.

Elizabeth chuckled. "Finally a reaction."

"Did you think we'd be surprised?" It didn't seem likely. Immediately after she'd rung to say she and Hari had something to tell us, Simon had bought the champagne.

"No, Mum. I wasn't expecting anything from you."

I've been very careful, always, not to show reactions to her boyfriends. I didn't want to interfere as my mother had. You see Mum hadn't thought much of Simon.

"He's nice enough," she'd said. "But not exactly going places, is he? Not like that Adrian."

I saw her point. Adrian did seem to have 'better prospects' and was certainly more dynamic. I'd taken Mum's opinion into account when both boys made clear they wanted more than occasional dates and I had to drop one of them.

Adrian gave me an exciting social life, a huge solitaire diamond, and my darling Elizabeth. Then, as Mum predicted, he went places. Places which didn't include me.

By the time Simon and I married, Mum had decided nice enough was good enough after all. They get on well now and I know she appreciates his steadiness and reliability. I like those qualities in him too, but I love him for a whole lot more.

Elizabeth has met Adrian numerous times and he's sent money for her, but Simon has always been her dad. I'm sure Adrian will get an invitation to the wedding. He might even pay for some of it, but Simon will walk Elizabeth down the aisle.

When Elizabeth was thirteen she announced she had a boyfriend. Simon fretted she was too young, but I persuaded him not to overreact.

"She's quite sensible and he seems nice enough."

That phrase of Mum's brought back memories and prompted me to hide my reactions to all of Elizabeth's relationships. With that first one they only sat in the park together, or went for a burger in town. If I'd been heavy-handed I might have pushed her into keeping secrets from us.

Staying quiet was definitely the right thing to do with Leo. He was dreadful. The result of Elizabeth's teenage rebellion. There were others. Some pleasant young men I'd have been fairly happy to have as a son-in-law, some I was frankly glad to see the back of. I never let my feelings show, beyond mopping her tears when needed.

Simon followed my lead by trying not to interfere, but

couldn't hide his feelings. Nobody was in any doubt as to which boys he disliked and which he might, grudgingly, agree were just about OK. Hari started in the latter category, gradually rising to become the reason for buying anticipatory champagne.

Mum learned to hold her tongue too, at least when Elizabeth could hear. At first she'd been wary of Hari's appearance, but has got to know him now. She'll be pleased about the engagement and will say so.

I felt Elizabeth squeeze my hand. How long had I been staring at her ring and looking into the past? She'd made her decision now and I'd accepted it. I could tell her what I felt without influencing her, without interfering.

"I like Hari," I said. "Elizabeth love, I've always wanted you to find someone who'd make you feel like I do about your father. Simon, I mean."

"I know," she said.

"Of course you do. And I know how you feel about Hari. I can see it in your face. In his too. How you look at each other. They way you reach for each other's hands and know, without looking, they'll be there. They way you laugh at silly things together." I said a lot more, but I'm sure you get the idea and more importantly, so did Elizabeth.

By the time we heard the garage door bang shut, we both had tears to wipe away.

I gave my future son-in-law a proper hug and could only hope he'd think that, as a mother-in-law, I was nice enough.

2. Perfection In Everything

Sapphire's footsteps slowed as she heard John's deep voice drift out into the corridor. Just being close enough for her ears to receive the caress of his words made her smile. It's said people never hear good of themselves when eavesdropping she remembered so sped up again, but not soon enough.

"I'm looking for the perfect woman," she heard John say.

"No such thing, mate," the voice of Rupert, Sapphire's boss, replied.

"There must be and she's the woman for me," John said.

Sadly Sapphire knew he wasn't talking about her, but at least she was reassured he hadn't yet found his perfect woman. She'd already decided he was perfect for her, so 'all' she had to do was to become perfect herself. The best way she thought, to discover what he felt constituted perfection, was to ask him. John was the same grade as her boss, but in a different department; a fact she used to her advantage.

"John, could I ask your advice?"

"Of course, Sapphire." He waved her into his office and invited her to sit down. "What can I do for you?"

"I'm thinking of trying to get promoted." Well, she had thought about it; mostly about whether it would allow her to spend more time with John.

John nodded encouragingly.

"Obviously I want Rupert to be impressed with me. What

can I do?"

"Be good at your job. Yeah, I know it sounds obvious, but that's what a boss wants. Other than that, reliability, being flexible and enthusiastic, willing to have a go, cheerful."

Sapphire thanked him extremely cheerfully. Although he'd been talking about work it seemed these were qualities he'd also appreciate away from the office. John took his job seriously and she was quite good at hers, so she should be able to manufacture plenty of chances to impress. Sapphire made it clear to both Rupert and John that she was willing to work in other departments whenever that would be useful. She increased the chances of John getting to see how good she was by putting a presentation together for the company. She volunteered for every training course going.

Every day, Sapphire took great care to look her best. She obtained a stylish yet practical wardrobe and hairstyle and made sure she always arrived in good time so as to avoid unprofessionally flustered entrances.

Her plans seemed to be progressing well when she was called into Rupert's office.

"Sapphire, we have a bit of a situation with the team-building event we're holding for new staff and I was wondering if we could persuade you to help out."

"Yes, Rupert?"

"There will be several young women attending this event and unfortunately, as yet, there are no women in management positions. We'd like these girls to have someone to turn to and a role model. It would help a lot if you could take on that position for the weekend. We'd give you a few days off in the week to compensate, naturally."

She was sure he was hinting the lack of a woman in a

higher grade was also something she could help redress. He wasn't to know that the hope of promotion wasn't the best way to motivate her. Neither was time away from the office, and therefore John. It would be a good way to show her flexibility and enthusiasm though and perhaps give him a chance to miss her smiling face?

"John Budd suggested you actually. He's heading up the event this year and as soon as the matter was raised he said he thought you'd be a valuable addition to his team."

Three whole days and nights away with John?

"I'd be delighted!"

Everything seemed to be falling into place until a couple of weeks later when she found out exactly what was involved on the course. It would mostly consist of sporting activities – and she'd have to join in.

Sapphire was reasonably fit because she did aerobics; at home from a dvd as she was completely uncoordinated. Even so, she always got really red faced and shiny looking. She wasn't good at any sport at all and would have said no, but that would have caused difficulties at that late stage. She must seem reliable.

She did her best to create a good impression from the start by arriving early with minimal luggage and greeting everyone cheerfully. She suggested she sit next to John at the front of the bus. "It might be best to let the others bond, without feeling we're watching them constantly."

"Great idea, Sapphire."

"Here's the itinerary of the weekend's activities," she said handing him a neatly typed sheet.

"Thank you. I'm sorry you had to redo it at the last minute."

"No problem." She'd been pleased bad weather meant the orienteering course had to be cancelled. Her sense of direction wasn't a strong point. That sense of relief lasted until she found it was to be replaced by indoor rock climbing. She'd seen from the brochure how attractive she'd look in that gear!

"Excellent," John said after reading through her efforts. "Shame we can't run off a copy for everyone."

"Oh, but we can. I phoned ahead and checked there was a computer and printer available at the activities centre."

"You really are the gem your name suggests, aren't you?"

She blushed. When they stopped for a break he took her off on her own for coffee.

"Let the others bond some more, shall we?" His grin as he said it suggested he was using that as an excuse in the same way she had.

That evening, when all the participants met in the bar for a drink, John sat close beside her. Sapphire was cheerful, very cheerful, but still behaved professionally and responsibly.

The following day, the two of them split up for the first of the sporting events, much to Sapphire's relief. He didn't see what a fool she made of herself over the archery and indoor kayaking. Luckily he couldn't see the chlorine she'd swallowed either, so she didn't have to explain a freak wave in the pool.

He did see her black eye though. Only Sapphire could elbow herself in the eye.

"Once again, you've done something I didn't think was possible." He said it so kindly and dabbed her face so gently with witch hazel she was sure he must really like her. Perhaps even enough to let him overlook this one imperfection? She could only hope.

John wasn't there to see Sapphire tangle herself in the volleyball net. She considered trying to use cookies to bribe the other players into silence, but decided that was probably unethical. There was no use her disguising the fact that many of her yellow team members ended up covered in yellow paint after the paintball battle, but Sapphire hoped John wouldn't realise it had all come from her gun in a moment of panic.

By lunchtime on the Sunday, it really seemed the team-building event was going to be a complete success. Everyone was working well together. The staff had all got to know each other and were developing good working relationships and learning to trust one another and use each person's strengths to the best advantage. When a couple of senior managers paid a surprise visit they were clearly impressed with how things were going.

"I reckon that promotion you wanted won't be long in coming, Sapphire," John told her.

She tried to look pleased, after all he wasn't to know that wasn't exactly why she was there. Right then, her career prospects seemed unimportant. Rock climbing was the last event and she had to find a way to survive it, preferably as far away from John's line of sight as possible.

"Sapphire, can I be your climbing buddy?" John asked.

She liked that he'd asked, but not that it meant she had to make her first climb right in front of him and he'd see exactly how big that harness made her bum look.

He misread the look of panic on her face. "Don't worry, I've done this before."

Great; he'd know exactly how bad she was.

He assured her the ropes were safe and she believed him. It didn't matter too much though. She probably wouldn't manage to climb far enough to hurt herself when she fell and the crash mats looked good and thick.

There was a warm up first, so she was red faced even before she started the climb. As she'd anticipated, she soon fell. What she hadn't expected was that she fell literally into John's arms with the wind knocked out of her.

She lay there, sprawled on the mat, bruised, red faced, sweating and hardly able to breathe.

"No, don't try to move," he told her when she tried to scramble to her feet.

"It's OK, I'm not injured." A jolt of pain shot through her and she yelled, proving that wasn't really the case.

"I think you've dislocated your shoulder," he said. "We're going to have to get you to hospital."

"I'm so sorry. I've made a perfect mess of things, haven't I?"

"You have, Sapphire. Of course you have. You do everything perfectly."

"I do?"

"Yes. Now do you have the strength for a perfect kiss before the ambulance gets here?"

3. Quiet

It was the washing machine that did it. The latest sound in what felt like a lifetime of noise. Susan had just sat down to have her lunch when it beeped to tell her the clothes were ready to be put out to dry. With a sigh she put down her fork and pushed back her chair.

"Leave it, love," George said.

"If I don't switch it off, it'll just keep doing it."

"Well ignore it while you eat."

"I can't! I can't ignore it. They're designed to get my attention and they do, even over the noise of next door's lawnmower and the scrape of your fork. Just as I hear the kids coming home at three in the morning despite your snoring and someone's dog barking. Just as I hear the oven timer ping over the TV and I hear the pedestrian crossing beep as I walk down the street and every shop plays awful music or irritating adverts or both and the …" She stopped aware that although she was dramatically increasing the household noise levels, her husband was tuning out her words.

"I never realised you were so bothered by my snoring. I'll see the doctor if you like."

"It's not just that and actually you don't snore loudly. It's no worse than a cat purring. It's just that it never seems to be quiet anywhere, ever." She went into the kitchen to turn off the offending washing machine.

When she returned to her husband and her lunch, she said, "Sorry about the rant. It's just because I can't get away from it. Noise, I mean, not your snoring. Even if I go for a quiet walk, just when I've got away from the rumble of traffic my mobile will ring and someone will tell me I've been mis-sold insurance."

"Yes, that is annoying, but I don't think you'd really enjoy total quiet."

"I would! You know I prefer to read instead of watching a film and turn off my mobile before picking up a book, even if one of the kids might call."

"True, but you encouraged those same kids to play noisy games and taught them ones you loved as a child."

"I suppose."

"And I don't remember you complaining about the din at the Saturday night disco."

She grinned. "No, it was always you who suggested going outside where it was quieter. Don't think I didn't know you had an ulterior motive."

"Of course you knew. That's why you were so quick to agree."

Pretending she'd not heard that she said, "OK, so I've not always been bothered by noise. Lately though I'm surrounded by it everywhere, all the time, and I want a break from it."

"You won't like it."

"I will, George! And what's more I think I need it."

"Then you shall have it, love. How about one of those deprivation chamber things? You just float in total silence."

"That'd be quiet, but claustrophobic too. Anyway it's only noise I want to cut off, not everything."

George booked a break in a remote cottage. When he stopped the car and got out, all she could hear was the sound of birds twittering as they settled into their roosts for the night. Even she couldn't consider that happy sound as noise. Besides, it would be dark soon and they'd shut up. Delicate flakes of snow swirled gently and silently down. The cottage had no electricity so there wasn't even the hum of a fridge to disturb the peace.

"This is perfect, George. Thank you."

"Glad you like it. Now don't forget to keep putting logs on the Aga. That's the only source of heat and you'll need it to cook too."

It was then she realised he'd only brought in her bags and boxes of books and supplies. His things were still in the car. "You're not staying?"

"No, love. Total peace you said and I snore remember?"

"I didn't mean …" She'd been about to say she didn't mean she wanted a break from him too, but it wasn't entirely true. With only George between her and perfect silence she knew him interrupting her reading for help with a crossword clue or to ask if it was teatime yet would really irritate her.

"What are you going to do?"

"I've booked into a pub in town for two nights."

"But the cottage is booked for a week."

"You'll soon be fed up with the quiet and want company," he said.

"What's that irritating noise I can hear?"

"Me being right." He kissed her. "Speak to you very soon."

"I'll see you in a week." She pulled out her mobile and made a point of switching it off. Then she hugged her husband. "I might miss you a tiny bit though."

Susan heated a can of soup on the wood burning stove and poured herself a glass of wine. Then she read a book straight through from cover to cover. She'd not done that since she was a schoolgirl and it rained during the holidays. When she reached the end, she piled logs onto the Aga and went to bed.

She woke with a start in total darkness. What was that horrible thudding? One of the kids come back late and fallen down stairs? She listened but there was nothing, not even George's snoring. Susan reached out. He wasn't there! The thudding got louder… then she remembered. No one had fallen downstairs because there were no stairs. She was in the cottage on her own and it was completely quiet, except for that thudding.

It was her heartbeat; definitely something she wanted to keep hearing. Once she realised what it was, it sounded reassuring, just like George's quiet snore.

Susan slept again until the sound of birds singing told her it was time to get up. She pulled back the thick curtains and saw a perfect, silent, blanket of snow.

She pulled on her dressing gown and went to the kitchen in search of tea. She had to coax the Aga from its overnight warmth into a fire capable of boiling water. The old ways of doing things weren't just quieter they were slower too but that was OK. She could read while she waited.

Without any noisy distractions Susan was soon involved in another story. At the end of chapter three, with the heroine running from the villain, her throat was dry in sympathy. Of course it wasn't just that, she hadn't had her morning tea either.

As Susan stood up she noticed an unpleasant smell. It got

stronger as she returned to the kitchen. The kettle had boiled dry! "Stupid thing. Why didn't you whistle or something to let me know you were ready?"

Then she laughed at herself. George was right, she did want some noises. She picked up her mobile. One of the sounds she most wanted was that of his voice even if it was to hear him say, "I told you so."

4. Waving Goodbye

"I have a surprise for you," Bert said.

Just for a moment, Marjorie experienced that once familiar feeling of disappointment, but history couldn't be repeating itself, not now. Bert had left the Navy more than twenty years ago. He couldn't possibly be about to go away on duty. He couldn't be about to sail into the sunset, leaving her waving from the shore.

"It can't wait until tomorrow?" she asked, wondering what difference a day could make.

"Not really, love. I know it's a day early, but I think we'd better open our presents today too," he gestured toward the pile of brightly coloured packages which had been accumulating over the last few weeks. They were golden wedding anniversary gifts from the couple's five children, their grandchildren, friends and neighbours.

"But I thought the children would be here tomorrow. Oh Bert, I'd hoped we would all be together."

Bert held his wife; he patted her back and offered his hanky to wipe her eyes. Marjorie knew he hadn't meant to, but once again, he had hurt her.

"They'll be here love, we'll all be together. You don't think I'd miss our golden wedding do you?"

Marjorie hardly heard his words, she was thinking of all the other important occasions he had missed. Well not missed, they'd always celebrated the anniversaries, the birthdays and Christmas. The turkey dinner might have been eaten in November, or February but they had always got together as a family whenever they could.

It had all started with their rushed wedding. When Bert, as a young able seaman, received his first sea draft, he decided he wanted a wife to come home to. He'd been shy and by the time he'd summoned the nerve to propose there was barely time to organise the ceremony. Instead of the romantic foreign honeymoon Marjorie had dreamt of, they'd had three days in Gosport. Bert's aunt had stayed with his mother and allowed them to use her house. Marjorie hadn't minded, being married to Bert was what mattered, not the location or length of their honeymoon. Watching the sunset creating gorgeous reflections on the sea together was romantic. What did it matter that the sea was the Solent and not the Caribbean or Indian Ocean? Marjorie was sure they would have plenty of chances to visit all the places she longed to see.

Marjorie had moved into their married quarter and got over the worst of her morning sickness by the time Bert returned. The first child was a boy, he was followed by a sister, two brothers and then another sister. Marjorie quickly realised that her dreams of foreign travel were destined to stay as dreams.

She watched her husband sail away many times. She would take the children down to old Portsmouth, climb the Round Tower and wave him off. She'd be back there, again, on his return. Was she jealous of his adventures? Not really, although she longed to travel, she wouldn't have traded her children for the chance.

Her three boys followed in their father's footsteps, by choosing lives at sea. One was in the Royal Navy, two were merchant seamen. She went to wave them off too, whether they sailed from Portsmouth, Southampton, Plymouth or Felixstowe. If Bert was home he'd come with her. When together they waved their first grandchild, their precious Angie, on her first trip, she thought Bert was beginning to understand the emotions she'd experienced so many times.

Marjorie wasn't jealous of the children either. Girls could go to sea now, have their career first and a family later, just as Angie was doing. Marjorie hadn't wanted to join the Royal Navy or serve on a merchant vessel. She knew there was a big difference between the life aboard a warship, oil tanker or container ship and going overseas on holiday. It was the romantic side of travel which appealed to her. The realities of a working life at sea held no interest. She did envy them the communication they had now though. Thanks to satellites and computers, families could stay in touch easily. There was hardly a day that need pass without a phone call or an '.

Marjorie remembered the weeks which had sometimes gone by without a word from Bert, then the joy when a whole packet of letters arrived. She'd read and re-read every one so often they had long ago worn thin at the folds. She still had them, still liked to look through them occasionally. In every one he told her that he loved her, wrote of the wonderful times they would have when he returned. He kept every promise. He'd told her too of the places he had visited, the strange plants and different foods. He wrote long descriptive letters, she almost felt that she'd visited these places too.

Four years ago, they almost went together to the first foreign port Bert had visited; Malta. They had got as far as applying for passports and collecting brochures, but then

Marjorie developed an ear problem and her doctor warned her that flying would be very painful. There would be no jetting off abroad for her now. There would be no more lonely weeks and months separated from Bert either; he was home for good. They were both in good health and she anticipated many more happy wedding anniversary celebrations to share.

So why did Bert want to open the gifts a day early? Why, if he had planned a surprise, must he tell her of it before the event?

"Come on, I'll pour us a glass of wine and we'll unwrap them together," Bert urged.

He took wine flutes from the cupboard and a bottle of sparkling wine from the fridge.

"That's for tomorrow," Marjorie said.

"No, love. This one's for tomorrow." He held up a bottle of real champagne. How had he got that into the kitchen without her noticing?

"Come on, indulge me," he coaxed. "You know, I always enjoyed those early Christmas parties, the times we celebrated birthdays and anniversaries in advance. I always felt like a kid getting an extra treat."

Marjorie smiled, he was right; they'd had some great parties, even if they had been at the 'wrong' time. If he wanted to celebrate their anniversary a day early, then that was fine with her.

They began to unwrap their gifts. The first was from their daughters, a joint effort and contained clothes. There was a smart charcoal grey suit for Bert, lightweight, but of good quality. A long velvet skirt was obviously for Marjorie. The colour was rich plum, there was a matching jacket too. She held them against her, confident that both the cut and shade would complement her perfectly.

"Well these are lovely, but rather smart for us, Bert. I'm not sure where we could wear them."

"Don't worry love, I'll think of somewhere suitable."

Marjorie thought she'd guessed Bert's surprise. He must be going to take her to a fancy restaurant. That would be nice. She liked cooking, but also enjoyed having food prepared for her and no washing up to do. Perhaps he would take her to the Italian place which had just opened? She'd hinted that the menu displayed in the window looked interesting. Bert didn't usually pick up correctly on her subtle hints, although he did try to decipher them. An Italian cookery book was as likely to be his interpretation as a night out. Marjorie shook her head; even Bert wouldn't expect her to cook pasta and rich tomato and herb sauce whilst dressed in flowing velvet.

The next gift was a set of toiletries, really good quality ones, and so many different things, all in tiny bottles and jars and packed into a neat bag. She would enjoy trying the luxurious items, although she wasn't sure how many of the creams and lotions Bert would be tempted to use. There were some peculiar gifts from their friends, a disposable camera, a swimming costume and pair of trunks, a tiny iron, a photograph album. She supposed that the two of them were rather difficult to buy for, as really they had everything they needed. The last gift was huge and from all the boys, it was a whole set of matching luggage.

"Bert love, what are we supposed to do with these?" Marjorie asked.

"Fill them with clothes, I imagine. All our best things."

"We're going away?"

"We are."

"Where?"

"Everywhere, love, everywhere," Bert grinned at her. "Finally, I can sail away and not leave you behind. I can show you the places I've told you about. Marjorie love, I've been saving for this for a long time. All the kids have contributed, even the grandchildren. We leave tomorrow on a round the world cruise."

The following day their family arrived, all their children and their partners, all of the grandchildren and a few cousins. Friends and neighbours crowded into the house. They shared a buffet lunch, before a convoy of cars set off for Southampton. Fifty years after she had married Bert, Marjorie stood on the deck of a luxury cruise ship and waved as she sailed off and others were left on the shore, watching and waiting for her return.

5. Losing Battle

"A pumpkin?" Linda asks.

"Yes," Sally replies.

"The enormous orange things you have at Halloween?"

"Yes, but smaller obviously."

"Oh yes obviously. We can't have the terrific Tim thinking you're odd!"

Linda makes a face at her friend from behind one of the display boards. The tourist information office is always quiet for the first half an hour or so in the mornings. The girls have time to chat as they replenish leaflets and check that posters are still in date.

"Sally, tell me again how a pumpkin will get you the perfect man."

Sally describes meeting Tim, her gorgeous new neighbour, at his housewarming party the previous Saturday. She had liked him a lot and thought that maybe he liked her too. He had seemed interested in her job, they liked the same music, and he'd even laughed at her jokes. For the first hour, he hardly left her side, but as more people arrived and the party warmed up his attention was constantly being claimed by others. Sally wasn't sure exactly how interested in her he was. Deciding that she needed another opportunity to impress him with her wit and personality she'd deliberately left her pocket dictionary as an excuse to return.

Late Sunday morning, after making more of an effort with

her appearance than she had for the actual party, she knocked on her neighbour's door. She was disappointed to discover that only Trevor, Tim's flat mate, was at home. Sally retrieved her dictionary but ensured she dropped a china fish. She called in to reclaim this after shopping for groceries the following evening. Again, Tim was out, so she accidentally left the pumpkin.

"A pumpkin though?" Linda asks.

"Yes ,clever eh?"

"How do you work that out?"

"Well it implies that I can cook, and at the party all the food was vegetarian. Vegetarians eat pumpkins and stuff like that."

"Perhaps, but why leave such odd things?"

"To make him curious about me."

Their conversation is interrupted by a lady searching for her missing umbrella.

"Take it everywhere I do, I feel quite lost without it."

"Can you describe it?" Sally asks.

"Black and … sort of umbrella shaped." She gives an apologetic shrug.

They have several umbrellas in the large cardboard box that is kept beneath the counter for lost property. Whenever anything is found locally it's usually handed into their office. If anything looks valuable or is unclaimed after a few weeks, it's taken to the police station. The girls look through the contents but none are claimed by the lady. Sally almost suggests the lady try the police station, but is interrupted.

"Never mind, it was a bit old and shabby, now I have an excuse to buy a bright new one."

"See what I mean?" Sally says. "If the umbrella had been interesting she'd have been more bothered about getting it back. As it was she probably only asked because she was passing anyway."

"That's not the same at all. You're losing things on purpose."

"Maybe she did too subconsciously because she wanted a new one?"

"Maybe." She doesn't look convinced. "Or maybe you're the only person in the world who thinks losing something is a good way to find something else?"

"Then I'm unique which makes me interesting!"

As Linda returns the umbrellas, an elderly man brings in a single black leather boot. It looks like the kind a soldier would wear, in fact this particular one looks like its owner had fought a war or two whilst wearing it. The man explains that he wouldn't normally have bothered with it but he saw a young man drop it. He'd called out to him, but had been unable to attract his attention.

"And I'm far too old to go chasing after careless kids these days."

Sally opens the door for the man, then waves the boot at Linda.

"See this, unlike the interesting things I've been leaving at Tim's flat, it's boring. Old-fashioned, dull, no one's going to wonder who lost it or want to meet them. Hardly the sort of thing you'd bother looking for either."

"Worse than a shabby umbrella?"

"Much. This is totally useless."

The boot is placed with the other items awaiting claimants. The phone rings; someone requires details of reasonably priced hotels, and bed and breakfast establishments. A list is promised and put in the post by Linda. Sally checks the emails and replies to most queries immediately. There is a complicated message about local history, this one is forwarded to the library; two of the staff there are keen on this subject and will be pleased to help. The post arrives before she finishes, she offers to help Linda in sorting it out but, before she can do so, a large lady dressed in a tweed suit and stout shoes arrives. In an accent remarkably like the Queen's she asks for directions to a local landmark. Sally follows her out of the shop, returning after a minute.

"I just wanted to see if she lives up to her image."

"And does she?" Linda asks.

"Absolutely, her husband, who has an enormous moustache by the way, was waiting in a large Range Rover with a couple of labradors in the back."

"You are nosy."

"No I'm not, I'm just interested."

The tweed wearing lady is the first of a steady stream of visitors which continues until well past lunch time.

Neither of the girls takes a lunch break, usually by midday the office is too busy for them to leave one person on her own. They wouldn't consider they were offering much of a public service if they closed just when they were most in demand. They took it in turns to run over to the deli to collect salads or bagels in summer and jacket potatoes in winter. It is Sally's turn today. She buys a couple of cakes too, it doesn't seem likely they'll get the chance to go out again this afternoon. Sally thinks Linda seems a little uneasy. As soon as the couple she is talking to have left, she asks for an explanation.

"A man walked by looking in the window, then he came back. After a while, he came in, then started asking if I was on my own here and what time I finished. He gave me the creeps."

"Why, what was wrong with him?"

"Nothing really, it was just odd. He didn't ask for information or even look at the leaflets. Just asked when you'd be back. Then I saw him watching from across the road."

She stops talking as a couple of middle-aged ladies wearing matching cardigans come in to ask if any private gardens are open locally.

"Preferably somewhere that does nice refreshments too."

"All that looking at herbaceous borders gives us quite an appetite."

"And a thirst."

They're given several leaflets for local gardens, parks and the botanic gardens nearby. They leave wondering if they have time to visit them all.

"Bet they have gin in their refreshments at each one if they do." To her surprise Linda didn't tell her off for being cheeky about the clients.

"Sally, that man, do you think he's planning a burglary or something?"

"Do you?"

"Not really, but he definitely seemed a bit on edge."

"Dangerous?"

"No, I wouldn't say so. Seemed odd though, him hanging round. He could have just been shy or something I suppose."

"Write down a description, and then if there's a break-in

we can let the police know. What did he look like?"

"Exactly like that," she muttered and nodded her head towards a man who was pushing open the door.

"Sally! Hi."

"Hi, Tim."

"Ah," said Linda, no longer nervous as his interest in the office was now explained. And if he was interested in her friend that went a fair was to explaining the fact he seemed a little odd.

"I was just wondering, has anyone handed in an old black leather boot?"

"Yes, I'll get it for you. Do you have the other one?"

"No, long story, I'll tell you one day. Can I take you out for a drink to celebrate its return?"

Two years later on their wedding anniversary, after eating a second helping of the pumpkin pie which Sally has eventually learnt to cook he tells her the truth. He bought two boots in a charity shop. He then dropped them separately in the high street to provide him with an excuse to see her again.

6. Eyes Down, Look In

"How's it hanging, mate?" Noah asked.

"By a thread," Alan answered.

"That don't sound good. The lovely Anne not succumbed to your charms yet?"

"No and there's not much chance she ever will."

"Don't put yourself down."

Alan shrugged. He was just being realistic.

"Ask her out," Noah urged. "If she's as nice as you say then she won't be single for long."

Knowing Noah was right, Alan decided to try. He 'accidentally' bumped into Anne three times but ended up doing no more than discussing the weather. On his fourth attempt she was with a man in a smart suit. Noah was right, he'd left it too late.

Noah was sympathetic when Alan explained. "Too bad mate, but I have some good news. There's a job going; cleaner and cloakroom attendant at the bingo hall if you want it."

"Course I do." Being unemployed was one of the reasons he lacked confidence.

A few weeks into his new job, a girl's locket fell off as she removed her coat.

"The catch keeps coming loose," she explained quietly.

"I'll keep it safe for you if you like," Alan offered. "Put it in here and write your name on the front." As he handed the girl an envelope, his mind was on Anne. He'd bumped into her as he'd walked to work. She'd seemed really pleased he had a job and hadn't mentioned the boyfriend. Perhaps he still had a chance?

It wasn't until the girl collected her locket that Alan glanced at her name: Geraldine Greenling. There had been a girl of that name at school and she looked about his age.

"Gee Gee?"

"I didn't think you'd remembered me, Alan."

He didn't, only how people used to pull her plaits as though they were horses' reins and tell her to giddy up. "Your hair's different, isn't it?"

She blushed and gave a shy smile which considerably improved her appearance.

"It suits you," he said, truthfully. Anything would have been better than tightly braided pigtails which made her seem to squint.

"Oh, thank you and thank you for looking after my locket for me. It was my granny's and means a lot to me." Her face got redder and her words faster as she spoke.

"No problem. See you next week maybe?"

"Yes. I come every week."

He'd been too busy thinking of Anne to notice.

Gee Gee often spoke to him, but unless he spoke first or prompted her it was no more than a whispered, "Hello, Alan."

If he asked questions she replied in a torrent of disjointed sentences. Alan recognised the symptoms. Her conversational style was very like his when he talked to Anne. Gee Gee was obviously shy, like him.

Knowing how painful it must be for her to make conversation, Alan helped as much as he could. His own shyness vanished whenever he saw her looking hopefully around and then a smile lighting up her face when he paid her any attention. Talking with him seemed to help her confidence. She stood taller, wore clothes which flattered rather than disguised her curvy figure and smiled a great deal more.

Alan noticed she no longer wore the locket.

"I daren't risk losing it," Gee Gee told him. "The catch on the chain isn't reliable."

He could see her point. Whenever he returned things people had dropped they always seemed amazed to get them back. He guessed not everyone was as honest as he was.

"Bring it in and I'll have a look. Maybe I can fix it for you."

She'd looked so happy. "Thank you, it would be wonderful to be able to wear it again."

When he left for the night and found a wallet in the street Alan's honesty was thoroughly tested. He flipped it open to check for identification. The first thing he noticed was a thick wad of bank notes. The second was a driving licence in the name of Philip Hedges. The photograph on that seemed familiar. He was fairly sure it was Anne's boyfriend. A further look revealed a picture of Anne herself, confirming his suspicions. Alan was tempted to give the wallet to Anne and say Philip had left it in the bingo hall. He'd naturally deny that, making Anne think he was a liar and causing trouble between them.

Better still, he could replace the photo of Anne with that of another girl. Maybe add receipts for a jewellery store or underwear shop. He'd make sure he was there to offer comfort to Anne when she learned 'the truth' about Philip.

No, he couldn't hurt her like that.

The following day was a Sunday, so Alan took the wallet to Philip's address.

He thanked Alan profusely. "Please come in. It's Alan, isn't it? You're an old friend of Anne's aren't you?" Annoyingly Philip seemed like a nice bloke.

"Er, yes. We went to school together."

"Come in, please. I'm sure she'd like to thank you, too."

Alan was reluctant. He thought it would be painful to see the two of them together.

By the time he was sitting on their sofa with a coffee he saw he was wrong. It was obvious the couple suited each other and Anne was happy. If Anne and he had been so well matched they'd have got together before now. Instead he'd used daydreams of something that could never happen as an excuse not to try to form a relationship with anyone else.

Before work on Monday, Alan visited the jewellers.

"Hey!" Noah's voice called out as he neared the hall. "How's it hanging, mate?"

"By a slender gold chain." One that would safely hold Anne's locket.

"What are you on about?"

"A girl I've got to know through work. This one won't stay single long either, not if I can help it."

7. Catching The 5.37

There was just a chance the train pulling out wasn't the 5.37 and she'd still be waiting. I kept running.

Emily. She's the reason I ran. Ordinarily I couldn't catch the 5.37, but sometimes it was late and I shared the journey with her. I like Emily a lot. She's the only woman I can talk to. Well, not only woman obviously. I speak to Mum and the lady in the newsagents and my boss. People like that.

I met Emily at my last job.

"There's no sugar left," she said as I approached the coffee machine.

I'd not really noticed her until then, at four feet three she's easy to overlook, but when she gave a shy smile I knew I wouldn't do so again. She's very appealing when she smiles.

"It's OK, I don't take sugar." Why did I say that? Of course it wasn't OK; not for her.

"Then would you mind programming a hot chocolate and we can swap?"

As I did, I kept quiet so as not to put my foot in it again and was rewarded with another smile.

She caught the bus right outside the building, I learned. Sometimes I waited there after work in the hope of seeing her before I went home. Is that weird? I hope she didn't think it was weird. Either way, it didn't do me any good as I never got up the courage to ask her out.

Three months after leaving the company I saw her again.

"Roger!" she called and waved across the train station.

It's hard to explain how pleased I was. To see her again of course, but even more because she'd chosen to be seen. You know how it is at stations, you keep your eyes down and don't engage with those around you.

She was on the platform I needed, so naturally I made my way over to her, but I think I would have done anyway.

"How are you?" she asked.

"Quite well thank you, and you?" Not an exciting line of conversation, but at least I spoke in a normal voice and didn't say anything stupid.

"Oh yes. I've got a new job. Applied right after you left."

We discussed the coincidence of bumping into each other. If her train hadn't been delayed due to a signalling failure it wouldn't have happened.

"I'm glad it was late," she said.

I was too. When it finally arrived we got on together. She was telling me about someone we used to work with, so to sit with her seemed natural. We continued talking, or rather she did. When nervous, people like me clam up, others talk. Emily told me she has two sisters, three brothers and a birth mark. She likes dogs, rainbows and cheese, can't play chess or the piano and carries a pen to correct ungrammatical signs. She got off at the stop before mine.

For the next few days the 5.37 had already left when I arrived at the station and I caught my customary 6.07. The next week Emily was waiting again.

"Engineering works," she informed me.

The hour long journey seemed to pass in minutes.

Over the next few weeks Emily reported more engineering works, problems on another route causing delays and staff shortages, as we travelled home. There was a piece in the paper about the train company winning an award for reliability. I cut it out for Emily. She chuckled as she read it.

"Leaves on the track," Emily explained when I saw her next.

"The wrong kind, I suppose?"

"Or the right kind, depending on how you look at it."

"I, er, yes it could be… it is a good thing… for me." If my face looked as red as it felt she didn't mention the fact.

The newspaper article got me thinking. I couldn't keep relying on delayed trains in order to see her. I asked my boss if I could sometimes work through lunch and finish earlier.

"I suppose so, if it's important."

"It is," I assured her.

"Oh?"

"There's a girl."

"Oh!"

She squeezed the details from me.

"Roger, catching the train isn't enough. You need to tell, or show, you like her."

"I have tried."

"Promise you will again and you can go early today."

Telling Emily how I felt was out of the question, so it had to be a gesture of some kind. Like flowers.

Carnations seemed too ordinary. Lilies spill pollen. A red rose was too definite a statement. I settled on freesias. They smelled good and I felt sure Emily would like them. The florist wrapped them nicely and attached a ribbon. I put them in my briefcase and set off for the station.

A glance at my watch showed I'd taken longer than expected, so I ran. A train pulled out. In the hope it wasn't the 5.37 and Emily would still be waiting, I kept running.

Emily was there!

"It's late again?" I gasped.

"Actually no."

I checked my watch. 5.39.

"I waited," she said.

"For the 6.07?"

"Kind of."

She'd waited for me. Emily liked me! With the running and the shock, or relief or whatever, my legs gave way. I sank down on one knee and put out a hand to save myself. Emily caught it.

We just looked at each other for… I don't know how long actually but we both realised at the same time that people were watching and pointing.

"They probably think you're proposing," Emily said.

"You're right. What shall we do?"

"People like romance, let's give it to them."

"How?"

"Ask me something I can say yes to."

"Will you come out to dinner with me tonight?"

"Yes."

I pulled her up and into a hug. The crowd cheered. I thought of kissing her, but didn't want to push my luck. That could wait until our date. Then I remembered the freesias.

"I got these for you."

The kissing didn't have to wait after all.

8. Thirty Years On

Edna loved her husband, but she'd had enough of Geoff's penny pinching ways and lack of romance. It was coming up to their thirtieth anniversary and she was determined he'd spend time and money on her, rather than his beloved garden. There was no way he'd come round to her way of thinking on his own. She'd need to devise a plan and then drop a hint big enough for him to notice. Hmmm.

"Geoff, I've decided. We're having a holiday this year."

"We are?"

"Yes. A proper one. Not a weekend break or visit to some relations, but a week in a nice hotel. Nearly thirty years we've been married and other than our honeymoon, we've never done that."

She had a point, he thought. They'd not been able to afford much when the kids were little, and he never wanted to leave the garden in summer. Edna had that determined look in her eye. Clearly he wasn't going to get away with it this time.

"Right you are, love."

Edna was slightly taken aback. He'd always managed to find an excuse before. Though to be fair, the last couple of years he'd had a proper reason; they'd been helping the kids set up home. "I'll have a think about where we could go," she said and went to make tea.

Geoff was thinking more about when. Not spring as he was too busy with seedlings, and not summer. September might not be so bad. The neighbours would water his plot in turn for helping themselves to tomatoes and beans. Prices were cheaper then too with children back at school. And their anniversary was mid September. He never knew what to do about that which upset Edna. Well, not this year.

"Edna," he called. "I've had an idea! Let's go away for our anniversary. We could go back to Harrington-on-Sea."

"Oh, Geoff, how romantic." She hugged him. "It's changed a lot I've heard, gone really upmarket, but I bet we'll find places we remember."

"Er, yes. I expect so." He dashed off to look up hotels on the internet. Maybe he'd get a discount if he booked early.

Edna was pleasantly surprised with his enthusiasm. She felt bad that she'd imagined him 'accidentally' not booking anything until it was too late, or trying to find a last minute deal somewhere awful. Harrington-on-Sea had featured in her magazine as being a preferred hideaway for quite a few A-listers. Her friends would be so jealous.

Really Geoff wasn't so bad. He often gave her flowers. Ones he'd grown himself, but wasn't that better than shop bought ones really? He always showed her the seed catalogues and let her select whatever she fancied. He wasn't like her friends' husbands, taking them to restaurants all the time, but that didn't mean he didn't love her. Geoff did things differently, that was all. Take her engagement ring for example. All her friends had diamond solitaires. There was hardly a difference between them. The stones in the ring Geoff had given her were the colour of champagne, or sunlight. Nobody else had a ring like that.

Geoff didn't like what he found on the internet. When they got married they could have bought a house for what it'd cost the pair of them to stay a week in the big seaside hotel now. In the end he found a guesthouse that looked quite like the one they'd stayed in during their honeymoon. It was still ridiculously expensive, but he supposed Edna deserved a bit of a treat. He'd never really spent much money on her and she rarely complained. Take her engagement ring for example. He'd got it in a charity shop. It was pretty though and Edna loved it despite it being so cheap. When he had the money, a good few years later, he'd offered to replace it with a diamond solitaire, but she wouldn't hear of it.

When they drove through Harrington-on-Sea Edna spotted the huge hotel right on the seafront. It did look plush, but it was the chain a lot of her friends stayed in. Somehow, despite knowing what Geoff was like, she'd hoped they'd stay somewhere she could brag about. That was selfish though, what mattered was that she and her husband enjoy themselves, not what anyone else thought.

It wasn't until Geoff said, "Here we are," she realised they were no longer on the seafront road, but outside a quaint old building. An exclusive boutique hotel! The inside was even better; real character and the ultimate in shabby chic.

Geoff was disappointed in the guest house. You'd think at the prices they charged that the chairs would match. Even the cups and saucers were a mismatch of the kind of crockery his gran had used for Sunday best. Edna didn't utter a word of complaint bless her. She even agreed it would be nicer to have fish and chips sat on a bench overlooking the sea than to go to the fancy oyster bar for supper.

"Just like we did on honeymoon! Lovely," she said.

He really was being so thoughtful. She'd walked up almost every street in the hope of catching sight of a celebrity and he'd not so much as asked what she was playing at. Edna was determined that Geoff would enjoy himself as much as she was, so suggested they visit all the local parks and gardens. She kept down the costs as much as she could too by filling a flask using the tea making facilities provided in their room before they set out each day.

Geoff was having a much better time than he'd expected. Edna seemed content to potter about looking at the outside of shops instead of dragging him inside, and they'd visited some lovely gardens. They'd seen Alan Titchmarsh recording for a show in one. Edna spotted him first and hadn't minded when Geoff stopped to watch. He chuckled, he might get her to watch the gardening programmes after this, in the hope of seeing themselves in the background.

They'd not spent nearly as much as Geoff had worried they would and already they'd been there six out of their seven days. Tomorrow was their anniversary; he'd splash out for once. Not go mad like, but he'd show Edna he wasn't always overly careful with his cash.

"Let's have a really good tea tomorrow love, remind us of our wedding reception."

"Oh, Geoff! Whereabouts?"

"Anywhere at all, love. Even that big swanky hotel if you like. You shall have the very best tea Harrington-on-Sea has to offer."

It'd cost a packet, but there had to be a limit to the price of a slice of cake and pot of tea that even the most expensive hotel could charge. Liked her cake did Edna.

On the morning of their anniversary, just as they were thinking of getting up, they heard a gentle tap on the door.

"Come in," Geoff said.

The landlady came in with a tray of tea and toast, plus a

tiny vase holding the rose Geoff had picked as a bud at home, and asked her to keep in the fridge ready for today. Shame that had made it a bit pale, but it was really nice of her to bring it in with breakfast in bed. Actually the service had been so good here he didn't entirely begrudge the bill which was coming.

Edna could hardly believe it. Most years she didn't even get a card, but he'd made up for it this time! Heaven only knew how much breakfast in bed was costing and that rose … it couldn't be coincidence. She'd chosen a bush for the garden which was close to the colour of the ones she'd had in her wedding bouquet, though just a touch too dark. This one was absolutely perfect.

They spent most of the day walking round Harrington-on-sea holding hands like newlyweds. Then Geoff had done the strangest thing. He'd suddenly pulled her across the road and stopped dead in front of a house, blocking the way of the man who was leaving. Edna couldn't think what he was doing until she saw who it was. Only the detective from her very favourite TV show! Even more astonishing, Geoff started a conversation with him and introduced her. Her hero had talked to her! Congratulated her on her anniversary! Given them a gift! Just think, for years to come she'd be able to casually mention to her friends that the rather attractive bush now growing in the garden had been a gift from him. True he'd simply agreed Geoff could take a few cuttings, but with his green fingers she knew they'd grow.

Bit of luck seeing that fuchsia, Geoff thought. He'd been after one like that for years. At first he'd thought it was bad luck seeing that chap come out, but really it was only right he should ask for a piece instead of swiping it. The chap had been quite charming and provided a knife, so Geoff was able to take several pieces and make good clean cuts. They were bound to grow. He'd go in the gents when they stopped for tea and wrap them in damp tissue.

Edna looked in the window of the fancy hotel. Gosh, they did champagne teas. Geoff had promised her the very best and that must have been what he had in mind. It was thoughtful of him but ... not really them. She'd enjoyed reliving some of the things they'd done on honeymoon, even though they'd had very little money back then. This didn't seem like the fitting end. And Geoff couldn't have the champagne as he'd be driving them home soon.

Geoff looked in the window of the fancy hotel. How much! Thirty-five euro for afternoon tea? Thirty-five euro each that was. What kind of place served champagne with afternoon tea anyway? Daft that was.

"Geoff, we've got tea in the flask. Be a shame to waste it."

He hesitated. "No cakes though. I promised you better than just a flask of tea."

"There's a bakery back there. Let's buy a few cakes and eat them on the beach."

"If that's really what you want?" He tried not to sound overly hopeful.

In the bakery Geoff pointed to each of Edna's favourites saying, "One of those and one of them and them," until she stopped him. She had to laugh when the salesgirl's, "Can I get you anything else?" was answered with a request for a damp tissue. He wasn't perfect, but he was her Geoff and she loved him very much. She told him so as they ate their lovely tea. "I know I moan at you sometimes for not being romantic, but really I'm glad I married you and don't regret a thing."

"Not even that engagement ring that isn't even a proper gemstone?"

"Especially not that. I love it and it's so unusual."

"You're telling me. When you said no to a diamond I realised you must like the colour and decided to get you a necklace with the same stones for an anniversary present."

"That was a nice thought."

"I did do more than think, love. I looked lots of places. Trouble was after spending time trying and failing to get you the perfect anniversary gift, most years I never got round to getting you anything."

"It doesn't matter." She tried to put real feeling into her voice, because really it didn't matter. Instead of hoping for a gift that would never come, she'd insisted her husband take her on holiday. And he had. They'd had a wonderful time. She didn't need, or want, more.

"Only way I could get one was to have it specially made," Geoff said.

Why was he still going on about a present? Then she saw the long thin box he was holding. She lifted the lid to see a necklace. Not just any necklace, but a unique handcrafted piece set with stones to match her engagement ring.

Seeing her reaction, Geoff seized his chance. "I was wondering about getting a greenhouse for the back garden. You wouldn't mind would you? I could grow much better fuchsias if I had one."

"Fuchsias? Is that what those cuttings we were given are?"

"Yes."

"I think a greenhouse would be an excellent idea."

It had taken thirty years, but finally she'd come round to his way of thinking.

9. What Use Is A Hen That Doesn't Lay?

Martha collected the eggs, all seven of them, and let out the hens, all eight of them. She wiped her eyes and blew her nose. Her nose ran because she'd just come out from the warm house, that was all. Martha wasn't crying. She definitely wasn't crying over some old chicken.

"What use is a hen that doesn't lay?" she muttered to herself.

There was no reply, because a non-laying hen was no use at all. Simple as that. Anything on the farm that was no use had to go. They were running a business, not a charity, as Joel would doubtless remind her if she suggested feeding an unproductive animal. He was right, they couldn't afford such sentimentality. Knowing it was true didn't help her like it.

Seven eggs a day was plenty. Enough for them and to sell a few to the neighbours. She should be pleased. She'd have been very pleased if they'd only had seven chickens. If it had been one of the others which had stopped laying it wouldn't have been so bad. Trouble was it was Chicklit. Martha knew it was her, there was no need to lift her up and feel to see if she was laying.

The hens all walked, one after another, down the ramp from their house and onto the bright spring grass. As always, Chicklit was first. Usually, the sight of her favourite hen leading the others out into the sunshine made Martha smile, but not this time. They pecked and scratched, oblivious to Martha's distress.

Martha's first project on the farm had been to raise hens. She'd not had much clue about anything on the farm back then in the first year of her marriage to Joel. She had known hens came from eggs though and had soon learnt about broody bantams and layers' mash and everything else needed to turn her dozen eggs into laying birds.

Chicklit had been the first to hatch. A tiny fragment of shell, like a pixie hat, had stayed attached to her head for a while.

Joel had said later, "You can't be sure which feathered hen was the first fluffy chick."

Martha did know. Even if she was wrong, she'd known.

Joel had been pleased when Martha raised eight hens to keep and four cocks to eat. Martha hadn't minded that the cocks had such short lives, not really. Or at least, she understood why that had to be the case. She tried not to think of the only possible use for a non-laying hen; chicken soup.

Joel hadn't let her name the orphan lambs destined to become chops and roasts, nor the piglets they were raising for pork. He'd known it would only make it harder for her when they had to go.

"We're keeping the hens though, aren't we?" she'd asked.

"Yeah. Suppose you can name them if you want."

She'd named them all for movie stars, all except her favourite. She knew Joel thought naming the hens was as daft as the romantic novels she enjoyed reading. He'd grinned when introduced to Chicklit, but said he liked red feathered Miss Johansson best.

"Her eggs won't be as good as Chicklit's," Martha predicted.

She was right. Chicklit was the first to start laying, just a few weeks later. Scarlett was last. Chicklit's eggs were the biggest and the most beautifully speckled. Even Joel had admitted as much. Martha wished now that hadn't been the case. Maybe starting so early and producing such big eggs had exhausted Chicklit. And maybe if her eggs hadn't been quite so distinctive, Joel wouldn't notice they were no longer being produced.

He would notice. On her birthday and their anniversary, he let her lie in bed until after she'd eaten the breakfast he'd prepared. Each time it had been the same meal. A pot of tea and jug of milk from their house cow. Bread made from their neighbour's wheat and baked by Martha the day before. A pat of butter she'd churned herself, and two lightly boiled eggs. Beautifully speckled eggs laid by her own hen. Martha's birthday was less than a week away. Joel would brew the tea, slice the bread and select eggs to boil. He wouldn't find the ones he'd be looking for.

There must be some use for a hen that didn't lay. Perhaps someone would want Chicklit to eat the slugs in their garden or as an unusual pet or mascot. If this mystery person wanted a hen at all, they'd likely want one that could lay.

Martha carried the eggs inside and added them to the tray in the pantry.

"You OK?" Joel asked when he saw her red eyes.

"Yes. Fine. Well, maybe a slight touch of hayfever."

"Thank goodness. With you gone so long and looking so sad, I was worried something had happened to Chicklit."

Martha just shook her head.

"Let's have boiled eggs for breakfast. We haven't had them for a while."

Of course they hadn't. Martha had served fried eggs or scrambled, poached or turned into omelettes. Anything so Joel wouldn't see Martha eating from a shell less heavily speckled than those Chicklit had laid.

"No, I've gone off them."

"Really, or is it because Chicklit has stopped laying?"

Martha just nodded. How had she expected to keep it from him? He was a farmer with a lifetime's experience. She'd only been tending animals for four years and she knew.

"Scarlett Johansson's eggs might not be as pretty, but they taste just as good."

"I know. I'm not really hungry, Joel."

"There is something wrong, isn't there?" He pulled her into his arms. "Come on, love. Tell me."

"It's Chicklit. What use is a hen than doesn't lay?"

Joel brushed the hair from Martha's face and kissed her forehead. "She brings a smile to my wife's face. What could be more important than that?"

10. Tender Touch

"Will you rub my shoulders love?" I'd asked my husband after a hard day at work on the cheese counter. I sat on the floor in front of David, so he wouldn't have to move off the sofa to reach me.

"I can't see the telly properly now, Diana," was all the reaction I got.

I don't really know why I'd hoped for sympathy, I rarely get it.

He rubbed my neck for about two seconds then said, "What you need is a cup of tea."

What he meant was, he wanted a cup, so why didn't I get him one and let him concentrate on the football.

I brought in the tea then rested my aching legs on the stool. David isn't any better at compliments than he is at sympathy. He never notices if I've had my hair done, but usually spots the things I'd rather he didn't.

"What's that?" he said, jabbing his thumb at the varicose vein beginning to form on my calf. "Not turning into Stilton are you? Better watch out or one of your customers is going to buy you by mistake."

"By mistake?" I asked, none too quietly. "Why 'by mistake'? Is it so impossible that a man could possibly be interested in me?"

"Steady on, I was just kidding," he said.

Next day at work, I was still feeling pretty fed up. My

shoulders were stiff, which didn't help. It was difficult for me to smile and be polite, but I did my best.

"Good morning, Diana, three ounces of Wensleydale please," one of my regulars said.

"Good morning, Malcolm." I tried to sound cheerful, but really, I just wished he hadn't asked for the cheese in the furthest, most difficult to reach part of the display cabinet. I felt a click in my neck and winced.

"Whatever's wrong?" he asked. Despite my pain I smiled. Here was someone who cared. He'd been kind before, I remembered. When I'd had a cold he'd recommended I drink ginger tea. I hadn't fancied that, but the ginger wine I bought instead made me feel a lot better. I told him about my aching muscles.

"You need someone to look after you."

I agreed. I didn't mention David; well he wasn't exactly tending to my every need was he? Other customers approached, so when Malcolm suggested we meet for a chat at lunchtime, I agreed without thinking.

He was very sympathetic. He said it wasn't surprising I suffered from aches and pains, as I worked in a refrigerated area.

"Muscles need to be warmed up before you use them; you're putting yours under strain."

What he said made sense. The company provides us with warm quilted jackets, but they're bulky and awkward to work in. Perhaps I should start wearing mine.

"Do you relax properly at home?"

I thought of David and his endless cups of tea. My expression must have told Malcolm all he needed to know. He said if I continued as I was, my pains would only get worse. He said I deserved to be without pain. He invited me round to his house that evening. I said 'no', of course. I went back to work and afterwards went home to my husband. I cooked his tea, which he gulped down before going out to play snooker. I took some paracetamol, tried to make myself comfortable on the sofa and wondered what would have happened if I'd accepted Malcolm's invitation.

The following week, when he bought more cheese he asked me to come to his house that evening. Again, I said no.

"I thought you'd say that." He smiled and handed me a folded piece of tissue paper. "Keep that with you. I'll be thinking of you this evening."

I slipped the paper into the pocket of my quilted jacket and forgot about it. As David slammed the door behind him on the way to snooker, I remembered it. Inside was a tiny crystal bead. I threaded it onto my necklace. I smiled as I thought of Malcolm.

The following week Malcolm noticed immediately that I was wearing it. David hadn't said a word, but Malcolm was delighted. When he again asked me to visit, I agreed. I know what you're thinking, but it wasn't like that.

David didn't notice that, after work, instead of changing into a saggy tracksuit, I put on smart trousers and my new sweater. He went to snooker as usual and as soon as he'd gone, I slicked on lipstick, added a squirt of perfume and went to Malcolm's.

He took me into a warm room, scented with perfumed candles. The low lighting and soft music were wonderfully relaxing. Malcolm was kind, gentle, caring. The moment his strong hands touched my aching muscles I felt the tension draining away. There are some who might say what

Malcolm and I were doing is not the proper way for a woman in my position to act, but I didn't care. It felt so good. I visited Malcolm every week after that.

Eventually David noticed a change in me.

"You seem less miserable these days. Your dodgy old legs feeling better are they?"

"A bit, yes."

"Why don't you come to snooker with me then? Do you good to get out."

I didn't think much of his idea of a treat. "No thanks."

"Got something better to do have you?"

"Anything would be better than sitting in that boring club watching you hit balls about."

David wasn't happy. I thought he wasn't going to go, but eventually I got him out the house and rushed over to see Malcolm.

I'd only been there a few minutes when the doorbell rang. It was David and he barged straight in.

"Who are you and what the hell are you doing to my wife?" he demanded.

Malcolm extended his hand. "I'm Malcolm Baker and I'm attempting to relieve your wife of the pains in her legs and shoulders."

"What?"

"He is healing Diana," Malcolm's wife explained. "He's a Reiki healer."

She handed David a leaflet. He glanced through it, before saying, "If you wanted your shoulders rubbed, why didn't you just ask me?"

11. The Gift Of Understanding

"Happy Easter, darling," Dominic said. He handed his wife a beautifully wrapped parcel. It was about the size and shape of an egg box.

Vickie gritted her teeth as she took the gift from him. It was heavy and by the feel she guessed it was six creme eggs. Vickie had always loved creme eggs; until she'd started her diet that was. She didn't need to look them up in her calorie list to know they weren't something she should be eating. It wasn't even as though she could just break off a small piece at a time. With a creme egg any normal person has to eat the whole thing at once. Any person with willpower like Vickie's has to eat the whole pack in a very short space of time.

Why couldn't Dominic understand that, although he'd given her chocolate eggs every year since they were together and she'd always enjoyed them, they weren't what she now wanted? He just grinned at her and waited for her to open the present.

She couldn't manage a grateful smile, but she mustn't start shouting at him until she'd at least checked to see what it was. She held the parcel still with both hands to prevent them shaking with angry frustration. She gazed down at the shiny paper and gauzy bow so he wouldn't see her disappointed tears. She wasn't upset because he'd given her an unwanted gift, but because he just didn't seem to understand her, no matter how carefully she'd try to explain.

She'd been slim when they met, well perhaps curvy was more accurate, but she certainly hadn't been fat. After they married, she began to put on a bit of weight.

"That's because you're contented," Dominic told her when she mentioned it. He seemed pleased to be the source of the contentment and clearly wasn't worried by a few extra pounds. Vickie had become pregnant and gained more weight.

"You're blooming, love," Dominic said as he gently caressed her belly.

She'd only shifted half the gained weight by the time she became pregnant a second time. Again she put on weight and failed to lose it all after the birth. By their tenth anniversary a friend joked there was two stone of Vickie that Dominic wasn't married too. She'd been upset, but Dominic had hugged her.

"Lucky me, now there's even more of you to love."

Her weight continued to creep up. She tried not to notice, or at least not to let it worry her too much. Most of the time she'd succeeded, until a month before Christmas. They'd been invited to a party and Vickie went shopping for an outfit. After visiting every shop in town, she'd been unable to find a dress to fit. She was used to having difficulty finding anything which looked good on her, but that year she couldn't even find something which would do up. She'd gone home in tears.

Dominic tried to comfort her. "Never mind love, those High Street stores just cater for skinny young things, we'll find you something on the internet."

They'd ordered a dress and gone to the party. Vickie knew she was the only one there who'd had to order her dress especially because no standard shop sold clothes large enough. The biggest woman there apart from herself was wearing a dress identical to one Vickie had tried and failed to squeeze into. She was quiet throughout the party and too upset to eat anything.

Back home, Dominic tried to understand. "It's true that you're not tiny, but what does that matter? In any group of people there's always one who's the biggest."

"Yes, and it's always me," Vickie said.

"Well I love you just as you are, and as long as you're healthy and happy I don't see that it matters what you weigh."

Vickie agreed with him, but as she wasn't happy, it didn't help. She knew she wasn't very healthy either. She got breathless walking upstairs, her hair and skin looked awful and she felt lethargic all the time. She went into the bathroom and eased out of the dress, vowing that never again would she have to order one from an outsize specialist.

That was another problem, here she was undressing in the bathroom because she was too ashamed of her body to let her loving husband see it.

"You can't really fancy me," she told Dominic.

He tried to prove her wrong, but she was too tired to respond.

Vickie knew that even if her wobbly bits didn't put him off, they were making her unhappy. She went to her doctor. He agreed that her weight was unhealthily high and gave advice.

"You're right doctor, but it's not easy to change my habits."

"Small changes can make a difference. Try to get some exercise every day, you don't need to join a gym, just do something that gets you slightly out of breath and keep it up for as long as possible."

Vickie giggled as she imagined explaining that one to Dominic.

Vickie followed the advice of her doctor and the dietician she was referred to. At the end of the first week she'd lost three pounds. She felt great. The next week she lost two more and was really pleased with herself. During the third week the novelty of all the salads and fruit began to wear thin.

"I really fancy some cheesecake," she told Dominic.

He went straight down the shop, saying he wanted the evening paper. He came back with a gorgeous portion of white chocolate cheesecake, "As a reward for doing so well."

She was a bit annoyed with him and really upset with herself for eating the whole thing as well as her proper supper.

To avoid too much temptation at Christmas she stocked the fridge with healthy food and didn't buy the usual boxes of shortcake, bags of nuts and tins of chocolates. Instead, she bought a few of Dominic's favourite nibbles and gave the children a selection box each. She was sure that if all the 'naughty' food was someone else's she'd manage to resist eating it. Her plan almost worked.

Dominic bought her an enormous box of Belgian truffles, some liqueur chocolates, a chocolate bar so large he'd needed two sheets of paper to wrap it and a novelty chocolate reindeer with jelly bean droppings. He also gave her what at first she'd thought was a set of towels and had been slightly annoyed at receiving something to be used by the whole family as a present. She'd been really upset when she realised the enormous mound of towelling was a single garment for herself; a dressing gown.

Vickie tried not to show how unhappy she was with the choice of gifts, but Dominic guessed he'd got it wrong. "Sorry love, I thought you deserved a few treats at Christmas."

"I know you were just trying to be kind, but I really do want to lose weight."

"I keep telling you, I love you how you are. You don't have to give up things you enjoy on my account."

"It's not just for you, I want to lose weight for myself too. I'm miserable as I am."

Finally Dominic said he understood and promised to help her. "Take the chocolates into work and share them out. I'll get you another present."

Dominic bought her a pair of running shoes and the whole family began taking regular walks together. At first Vickie tired quickly, but gradually began to go a little farther each time. Her confidence went up as her weight crept down.

"You look even better than you did five years ago and I certainly can't complain about your increased energy levels," Dominic remarked in bed one evening.

That's why Vickie was so upset at the gift he'd just given her. He understood that she wanted to lose weight, she was doing extremely well, but still had more to lose. He'd agreed to help and could appreciate the difference it was making, so why on earth was he giving her chocolate eggs? If he'd wanted to give her a gift why not flowers or a basket of fruit? Perhaps it was a test of her willpower? Well, she could do without that. Maybe he'd got fed up with her and this was his way of saying she might as well give up trying to be attractive as no one would want her.

Vickie took a deep breath, better get this over with. She tugged at the pale pink wisp of ribbon and let it fall. She undid the paper and revealed an egg box. A real one. She opened it. Inside were six kiwi fruit. She looked up at Dominic.

"I didn't want you to feel you were missing out when the kids ate their chocolate ones."

Vickie hugged her husband, then whilst the kids went to their grandparents for an egg hunt, she and Dominic burnt up a few more calories.

12. It's Just Not Fair

"Is that what you meant to do?" Wendy muttered at her colleague's retreating back. "Leave me stuck with Halitosis Harry?"

Just seconds before, Ruth had 'nipped out for a quick ciggie'.

Putting on her bravest smile and loudest voice, Wendy greeted Harry Russell.

"I can't hear you, dear," the man said, moving closer. He caught hold of her arm and put his face right in front of hers. "I'm getting a bit deaf," he confided, giving her a massive sample of his halitosis along with his camera's memory card. "Lovely snaps of the grandchildren here. You'll do your best with them, won't you dear?"

Wendy assured him she would as she took his money. After that she was alone for a few minutes. No customers, no Ruth. There was plenty of work to do though, as they were part way through the quarterly stocktake. Wendy picked up the clipboard, noticing considerably more than half the entries were in her own handwriting. Of course they were. Whenever it was quiet enough for them to get on with the job, Ruth had gone out for another 'quick ciggie'.

Thinking about it, Ruth always disappeared at a convenient moment – convenient for Ruth that was. She somehow managed to take a break whenever a particularly large delivery of camera equipment or an annoying customer arrived.

Wendy moved over to count the carbon fibre tripods in the window display. A man she recognised glanced in as he walked by. They'd shared a table in the busy sandwich shop last week, but before they'd done much more than agree the food was good and the weather bad, his phone rang. After glancing at it, he said he had to leave.

"Maybe see you around, if you work locally?" he'd said.

"I do, just over there," she'd pointed in the direction of the camera shop. Unfortunately she'd not seen him again since, not until now.

If Ruth hadn't been out smoking, Wendy could have taken her lunch break and engineered another 'accidental' meeting. Instead she advised a woman who was looking for a simple to use, inexpensive camera to take on holiday.

"If it's too fancy I won't be able to understand it and I'll just be worried about it getting stolen."

The man from the sandwich shop came in. He waited patiently as Wendy unboxed camera after camera for the lady to inspect. After looking at a few options, and asking a great many questions the lady said, "I'll have a think about it and come back later."

Wendy beamed at the man and was just about to ask how she could help when, right on cue, Ruth returned to the shop. "You might as well go to lunch now, Wendy."

Was it her imagination or did the man look disappointed? Wendy went over to the sandwich shop, but he didn't join her there and she didn't see him again as she wandered around town.

Ruth took her own lunch break as soon as Wendy returned. "This needs developing," she handed Wendy a roll of film and a receipt.

"He's paid for an hour's turn around."

"Yep," Ruth agreed.

"An hour ago."

"Really? Oh dear I've been so busy …"

Wendy didn't argue. For one thing arguing with Ruth was pointless, she always got her own way. Even when Wendy pointed out to Leonard Cappe, the area manager, that Ruth took extra breaks because she kept going outside to smoke the only action taken was for a small shed to be erected so Ruth didn't have to get wet whilst smoking. Naturally that meant she was in even less of a hurry to get back to work. Wendy's bitter thoughts were cut short when it occurred to her that an hour ago was just when the man from the sandwich shop had come in. He'd be back soon and Ruth would be absent.

She processed the film as quickly as she could. The resulting prints were far too dark. Now almost everyone used digital cameras, the film developer was rarely used. Maybe the machine wasn't working properly. Wendy adjusted it and tried again, but it was no good; the pictures simply hadn't been taken correctly. All were under exposed to some degree, many were out of focus and she was fairly sure a few had been taken unintentionally. Worse still the pictures showed what were probably his wife and children, so Mr… she checked the paperwork… Mr Peter Woodman was unavailable. Oh well. She'd obviously read far too much into his innocent conversation.

Wendy selected stickers for the worst of the prints and attached such useful advice as, 'This shot is very dark. A longer shutter speed or higher ISO would correct the problem'. Customers often appreciated advice on improving their pictures and providing it was something that earned the shop repeat trade.

Wendy was almost finished when he returned. "Hi, I've come for my photos. Peter Woodman."

"Almost done." Wendy gave him her brightest smile.

He didn't smile back. "They should have been ready by now. It's not right to charge extra for an express service if you can't provide it."

He looked and sounded just like the man she'd met before but he certainly didn't act like him. In an attempt to placate him, Wendy refunded the difference between the express and standard service, even though the standard service was a two day turn around and she'd kept him waiting for under three minutes – less time than if she'd been serving someone else when he'd returned. He took the money and pack of photos without a word of thanks. Wendy's jealousy of the man's wife was instantly replaced by sympathy.

That afternoon Ruth returned from yet another smoke break just as the woman who'd been looking for a holiday camera returned. "Whose turn is it to make the tea?" Ruth asked.

"Yours," Wendy said.

"OK," Ruth agreed, presumably happy to avoid the customer.

The indecisive customer again handled several cameras and asked multiple questions. She shook her head. "I'm so sorry, I still can't decide."

The following day Mr Cappe came for his regular monthly visit. While he was there Peter Woodman returned.

"Why are all these stickers on my pictures?" he asked.

Wendy tried to explain.

"Don't you think I can see they're dark? The haven't been

processed properly and you're trying to pass the blame."

Ruth stepped in before Wendy could utter a word and offered the man a full refund.

"There was nothing wrong with how I processed them," Wendy fumed to Mr Cappe. "He had no reason to complain."

"He didn't seem to agree with you," her boss pointed out. "Do you make many processing errors?"

He kicked his foot against the bin that still contained Wendy's first attempt at Peter Woodman's prints. Ruth had said she'd clear up the shop last night if Wendy did the banking. Clearly, and not for the first time, only one girl had carried out her part of such a bargain.

Just then the time-wasting holiday camera woman came back. Wendy couldn't sneak out for a cigarette break, but there was one way she could leave the shop floor. "Excuse me, I need the toilet."

She returned to the shop just in time to see the lady leave with two carrier bags.

"She couldn't decide which to get so she bought one model for herself and another for her husband," Ruth informed her.

The area manager praised Ruth as an excellent saleswoman.

As the perfect end to the day Peter Woodman returned with a huge bunch of flowers and an apology – both claimed by Ruth of course.

"I'm so sorry I was grumpy earlier. I found my granddad's old camera… he died recently. I was disappointed that his last photos weren't good. It's difficult for me to recognise my own sister and her kids in them, but he wasn't well …"

"That's OK, I understand," Ruth simpered.

"No excuse for my outburst though. I've just quit smoking so I'm a bit tetchy."

"I can understand that too! My colleague Wendy here," she jabbed a finger at Wendy, "is always moaning about my smoking breaks and saying I should quit."

"She's right," Peter said. "It's very unhealthy. Granddad died of lung cancer."

Neither girl said anything.

"I see you both agree. Tell you what, Ruth to make up for some of your smoke breaks you could let Wendy finish early and come for a drink with me. That's if you'd like to, Wendy?"

"I'd love to," Wendy said. "You don't mind if I finish a bit early just this once do you, Ruth?" She fetched her bag and coat without waiting for a reply.

Ruth didn't get the chance to say anything when Wendy returned to the shop floor either, as Halitosis Harry had arrived. He took hold of Ruth's arm and broke into a coughing fit. His hearing aid was making the kind of screeching whistle that suggested conversation would be very difficult.

Wendy could feel her colleague glaring at her retreating back and guessed the other girl was thinking, "Did you mean to do that?"

13. Listen To Me

"So, how did it go, Greg?" Lisa asked her husband, as he let himself into the house.

"Yes please, love," he said. He noticed her puzzled expression. "Sorry, I was thinking about my writing group. The speaker was really interesting."

"Oh, you listened to him, then?"

"Of course. Writers have to listen all the time; that's one of the things the speaker was saying. Ideas can be anywhere. I don't know where you get the idea I don't listen."

Lisa shrugged. "Would you like some tea?"

"Yes please, love," he said very slowly and carefully, to make sure she understood him this time. Again he noticed her expression. "I'll make it shall I?"

He handed Lisa the leaflet he'd been given about finding good subjects to write about and wandered into the kitchen.

Lisa read it. He'd been right; it did say that writers should listen. It also said that ideas which sounded exciting might not be and that sometimes it would be better to choose a less obvious subject. The sheet quoted as an example the horrendous sounding medical condition, pityriasis rosea and a small plastic clip; which would the group choose to write about? The leaflet pointed out that the medical condition was really a harmless rash, whereas the plastic clip played a vital role in keeping aircraft in the sky. At first glance, the clip might not have looked promising, but it might well provide inspiration for a dramatic story.

"I can't wait to get started on my next project," Greg called.

"What is it?"

"We were given a list of words to pick from and write a story about. Most of us didn't know what any of them meant, but he said that didn't matter, we could research them."

"What word did you choose?"

"That's where I was clever," he said like an author nominated for the Booker prize. "The list was divided into medical conditions, plant names and different types of plastic clips. Which do you think I chose?"

"Was one of the plants something poisonous?"

"No. I didn't think of that."

"The clip was stolen by an industrial spy and used to fund an evil empire?"

"Um, no."

"A new cure for cancer?"

"No," Greg sounded slightly annoyed. "I selected a medical condition. The speaker mentioned something about that earlier and straight away I thought of someone with a life-threatening condition who has a large family to provide for. He'd be rushing for treatment and there'll be a disaster and he nearly won't make it. Then there'll be an extremely tense surgical scene and then a touchingly emotional one as his family wait for the news."

"That does sound good. What's the condition? Maybe I can help with the research?"

"Thanks, love. I knew you'd want to help, that's why I chose the condition I did. I remember you talking about it.

There's no point in having a pathologist for a wife if I don't use her experience in my writing, is there?"

"I'd have thought there were plenty of advantages to having me as a wife, whatever my profession and your hobby," Lisa said that at a volume that even Greg couldn't avoid listening to.

"Yes. Sorry. Anyway, the point I was trying to make, is that you'd told me about this condition and I listened."

Lisa smiled. "Sorry, I didn't mean to snap; it's just that sometimes I feel you don't take any notice of me and the real world because you're too busy concentrating on your stories."

They hugged and sat quietly for a while drinking their tea.

"So, what's this medical condition, then?" Lisa asked.

"Lipoma. Do you remember telling me about it?"

"Yes, I do. Do you?"

Greg heard the warning in her voice.

"Of course! Well, not all the details. Perhaps I could ask you a few questions?"

"Yes. Why don't you write down the answers so I know you're paying attention?"

"OK." Greg fetched a pen and notebook. He felt guilty, he remembered Lisa saying the word, 'Lipoma'. He'd been attempting to write poetry at the time and guessed his mind had wandered away from what she was saying and he'd been trying to find rhymes. Oklahoma would work. Oh dear, he was doing it again.

"Sorry. So it was one of the bodies you were examining that had this?"

"No, Greg. It wasn't. It was me; still is."

Greg felt sick. Lisa had mentioned she'd found some kind of small lump a couple of months ago. He'd thought she'd said it was nothing. How could he not have listened about something so important? He took a deep breath.

"What's the cure?"

"Usually there's none."

"But, I …"

"You weren't listening when I told you about it, were you?"

Greg shook his head. "I'm really sorry, love. It's not that I don't care. Please tell me about it now. I feel terrible that there's something wrong with you and I didn't take any interest."

"It's nothing really."

Greg relaxed a little; he'd thought that's what she'd said. "Are you sure?"

"Yes. I knew what it was because of my job, of course, but most people would want to see their GP to get a diagnosis." She explained the lipoma was really just a fatty lump which rarely caused a problem or required treatment. It was all reassuringly dull until she mentioned them becoming cancerous.

"Cancer?" Greg's concern for his wife cancelled out his excitement over a possible story line.

"It's not at all likely. Some experts think it might be possible, but there isn't any evidence it's ever happened. Sorry, that's not much good is it?"

"Of course it is; it's excellent news. I wouldn't want you to be in pain or needing treatment or anything."

"Thanks, Greg, but I meant for your story."

"Oh. I see what you mean. Are they rare? Maybe I could make something out of that."

"They're quite common I'm afraid. That's not helping is it?"

"No, it's no good at all. Can you imagine it? 'Once upon a time our gallant hero got a lipoma, it was nothing to worry about, so after popping in to see the doctor to get it checked, he carried on just as usual. The End'. That's not very exciting is it?"

"Not yet, but what difference did the visit to the doctors make? Maybe he saw something on his way back to work that he wouldn't have otherwise witnessed?"

Greg and Lisa discussed possibilities. Greg listened carefully to every suggestion and eventually wrote an exhilarating story about a man whose visit to the doctors meant he saw a gang go into the bank and take the entire staff prisoner. The gallant hero rescued them all and foiled the evil gang.

"So, how did it go, Greg?" Lisa asked her husband, as he let himself into the house after the next writing group meeting.

"Brilliant. They couldn't believe that I'd managed to get a story out of such an uninteresting subject. I told them how it was all due to listening to my wife. Not that your great story ideas and help with research are your only good points off course."

"Did I hear that right?"

"Shouldn't think so, you never listen to a word I say." Greg winked as he said that and quickly offered to make the tea.

14. Looks Familiar

A mutual friend introduced Danny Walters and Sally Higginbottom. He'd stammered and blushed until she'd eventually coaxed him into asking her to dinner.

Other than thanking her, three times, for agreeing to come, asking which wine she'd like and placing his order, Danny said little. He fiddled with the pepper grinder, rearranged his cutlery and topped up her still full wineglass. "Are you sure this is OK? I'll order champagne if you prefer." He spilt some. "Sorry… I'm not usually this nervous."

"Is it because you're still thinking of me as Gemima Randolph?"

"Gosh, no. No way would I have been able to ask her out! Not that you're not as good as her …"

Sally reached out to squeeze his shaking hand. "It's OK."

"It's just that you're beautiful and successful and I'm so ordinary."

"I'm an ordinary person too, Danny. Everybody is really."

"I suppose you've met lots of famous people and know what they're really like?"

"Quite a few."

"How did you get started in your job? I see you're perfect …"

"Excuse me," a woman asked. "But you're Gemima Randolph, aren't you?"

"No, I'm her double and impersonator," Sally explained.

"Oh, right. Sorry to have bothered you." The woman moved away.

"That's how," Sally said. "I was in a restaurant and the man who now acts as agent for both of us heard me tell an autograph hunter I wasn't Gemima, just looked like her. He suggested I become her double."

"Very enterprising of him. Two clients for the price of one."

"That's exactly what he said. Now, tell me how you got into teaching."

Danny grinned. "I just like being the cleverest kid in the class."

As he described his work and young pupils, enthusiasm replaced his nerves. Sally thought he must be a very good and popular teacher. She also thought he'd make an excellent husband for the right person. Someone a lot like Sally Higginbottom.

Danny stumbled over his words as he said goodbye, but found the courage to kiss her cheek.

They chatted quite easily by phone several times and he didn't need much prompting to ask her on a second date. Again he was nervous to start with, but by the time another diner interrupted, he'd began to relax.

"You're that Gemima Randolph. I want your autograph."

"Actually I'm not Gemima, my name is …"

"If you're not her you shouldn't dress and act like her!"

Danny pushed his chair back and stood.

Sally put out a hand to stop him.

"Gosh she was rude!" he said after the woman flounced

off. "Do you get that a lot?"

"Not actual rudeness, but people usually lose interest once I say I'm not Gemima."

"That must be horrible."

"Not really. At least they see I'm a person, not just an actress or sometimes the character currently being played, which is how they think of Gemima."

"I read she sometimes hires you to attend award ceremonies and autograph sessions on her behalf …?"

"I couldn't tell you that, could I?" Sally winked. "But I think you can understand why she might sometimes want a break from the public."

Danny was less flustered as he kissed her goodnight for the second time, and soon rang to suggest another date. "We could try to find somewhere you're not likely to be recognised."

"I'd like that. What kind of things do you like doing?"

"Looking round castles and ruins, but you'd probably find that dull."

"I might not."

"Because you're an ordinary person?"

"Because you'd be there to make it interesting."

At the remains of a local tower he described the lives of those who'd once lived within its fortified walls. If Sally's teachers had been like Danny she was sure she'd have got a A for history. She was fascinated by his explanations until rain sent them rushing for the coffee shop.

As they joined the instant queue, Sally became aware of people staring and half whispering, "Is it her?'"

"Looking like that? Shouldn't think so."

"Bet it is. Get a photo. You could make some money."

Danny, said loudly, "So, Sally what would you like?"

The whispers and attention ended abruptly.

"Thanks," she muttered.

When they were sitting with their drinks, Danny said, "People are so horrible, aren't they?"

"Some people are sometimes horrible. Some are just ordinary like me and some are lovely like you."

Danny almost tipped his coffee into his lap.

Over the next few weeks, Danny and Sally shared meals, met for drinks and visited local landmarks. Danny addressed her loudly by name whenever anyone seemed to be paying them any attention. That usually meant they were left alone.

One day as they climbed a castle's spiral staircase a girl's excited words travelled up. "Mum! Mum! That was Gemima Randolph! Can I go talk to her?"

"She's with her friend, love. It would be rude to interrupt."

"I suppose …"

An hour later they were aware of a small girl doing her best not to stare.

Sally waved and the child rushed up pleading for an autograph.

"Sorry, she's a huge fan," the mother said.

"That's nothing to apologise for." Sally produced a photo of Gemima from her bag and signed it for the child.

"Is that your boyfriend?" the girl pointed to Danny.

"Yes, but it's a secret, OK?"

"OK. Can me and Mum get a picture with you?"

Danny took one on the mother's phone.

"You made that kid's day," he said afterwards.

"You think I should have said I wasn't Gemima?

"No… She could have met you when you were standing in and you'd have had to do the same thing then."

"But …?"

"Should you have said I was your boyfriend?"

"Well, you are."

"But not Gemima's They might talk about us."

"Maybe. Danny, I'm sorry but if you keep going out with me, you're going to see your picture in all the papers."

He shrugged as though it didn't matter but she knew how much such a shy person would hate that; probably as much as she'd hated keeping the truth from him.

"Danny… Everything I told you about being Gemima's double is true, but I left out the fact I'm really her as well. I lived a double life to try to get some privacy."

"Oh… I… oh."

Sally decided to let him get over that shock before hinting she was ready to give up acting and become someone else entirely – Mrs Danny Walters.

15. A Changed Woman

Julie's hair was looking good; shiny and neat. I almost made the mistake of mentioning it – or, I wondered would it be a mistake not to? I thought she'd been to the salon. If she had then I'd be expected to notice, but if she hadn't then I'd be accused of sarcasm or suggesting she should get it cut. Even worse was the possibility that she'd had it done last week and I'd only just realised.

I remembered the days when if my wife looked good then I told her and she was pleased at the compliment. Then she had the kids. Her weight went up a bit, she didn't have the time to get her legs waxed and polishing her nails was a waste of effort. She lost some of her confidence and thought she looked frumpy. I thought she looked beautiful. The extra pounds suited her and she was beautiful with or without make-up. Somehow I couldn't explain that to her. I suppose I didn't try hard enough. I'm always afraid to say the wrong thing so don't say anything at all. Better put that right, I decided.

"Your hair suits you like that, Julie, love," I said.

"You didn't like how I had it before?"

I sighed. Why had I bothered?

"Sorry, Callum," she said. "Of course you hated it before; it was a mess."

"No, I didn't mean …" Hopeless. How had we got to this state?

I didn't give up though. At the weekend I thought I'd try to bring some romance back into our lives and crept downstairs to brew coffee and toast bread. I thought breakfast in bed might make her smile. As I tiptoed along the landing, I heard her voice. She sounded upset.

"He can't even bare to face me in the mornings now. He's got out of bed before I'm awake."

There was a pause.

"Maybe."

Another pause.

"I'll try. Bye, Suzie."

I could only hope her sister hadn't been advising her to divorce me. I'd have taken the tray away, but our son saw me outside the bedroom and came and opened the door for me.

"Why are you having breakfast in there?" he asked.

"Because I want to spend some time alone with your lovely mummy," I answered loud enough for Julie to hear.

She drank the coffee and tried to smile. I drank mine, ate the toast and tried not to see her tears.

For a few days after that, she seemed happier. I noticed she had some colour in her cheeks. That told me how pale she'd become. I hadn't noticed. We'd drifted further apart than I'd realised. It seemed I hardly knew my own wife.

As the weeks passed, I understood how much had changed. She stopped joining me for a beer and crisps while I watched football and went upstairs alone to watch a video. Instead of me dropping the kids at school on my way to work, she said it would be better if she walked them there instead. She opened her own bank account instead of paying for the things she wanted from the joint account. It was as though she didn't need me anymore.

Julie started wearing clothes I hadn't seen before.

I overheard more snatches of conversation between her and her sister. She mentioned a man I didn't know; Paul Newman. She definitely wasn't talking about the actor. This bloke sounded extremely lively. Big changes and fresh starts were a feature of these conversations. I tried not to listen, but I couldn't help torturing myself. A fresh start without me, is that what she meant? Maybe his name wasn't Newman, she meant he was her new man? Did she want a change from me?

I had to take action. I'd show my wife I loved her and hope it wasn't too late. I booked the afternoon off work and bought wine and flowers on my way home. There was a car I didn't recognise outside the house. One of the neighbours must have a visitor.

Quietly, I let myself in. In the hall was a large case, with 'Paul Newman' stencilled on the side. I could hear music coming from upstairs and followed the sound. Our bedroom door was open. On the bed where the clothes Julie had been wearing when I kissed her goodbye that morning.

Kneeling on the floor outside the spare room I squinted through the keyhole. I saw my wife's bare legs stretched out, a strange man's hands on her thigh. I heard her groaning and watched the sweat trickle down between her breasts. I crept away.

Downstairs, I put the wine in the fridge and hid the flowers in the garage. It would give the neighbours something to talk about if I'd carried them out again. I drove to the end of the street and parked. I decided that once he was gone, I'd give her half an hour to shower then go back.

I knew Julie would still be surprised to see me. She'd be even more surprised when I told her I knew what was going on. I'd give her the flowers, but not the champagne and chocolates. If she wanted a fresh start, then I'd let her have one.

After twenty minutes or so, a man carrying a large case came out of my house and got into the strange car. I didn't notice the sign-writing until he drove by. "Paul Newman, fitness instructor. Newman can make you a new woman."

I went home to my wife. She wasn't a new woman. She was back to being the slim and confident woman I'd married.

16. For The Love Of Fennel

"... I'll bring Jacob to lunch on Saturday." Fennel disconnected before I could reply.

Probably just as well. I thought her boyfriend was a bloodsucking lowlife, nowhere near good enough for my darling girl. Not that I'm in any way biased.

"Isn't she coming?" Sharon asked from the kitchen doorway.

"They both are."

"Lovely!" she returned to her sanctuary, undoubtedly planning the menu.

I hoped it would include plenty of garlic. That might wake him up a bit. Jacob seemed to sleep most of the day. I really didn't want to think about what he got up to at night. I hadn't exactly met him but knew enough to heartily dislike him: Fennel says it's serious.

We arranged to have supper with the two of them one evening, but a puncture delayed us. There was hardly time for introductions before he had to fly. He dressed smartly, I'll give him that. His dark hair was tidily cut and brushed, his pale skin clean looking. He gave a nervous smile as though he had something to hide and shook hands with an icy grip.

"He worries me," I confided to Sharon.

"Everything to do with Fennel worries you."

That used to be true, but I'd got over it. I worried when

Sharon was pregnant and had high blood pressure. I worried about Sharon's health too, but that little scrap of life inside her seemed so fragile.

When Fennel was born early and had to be hooked up to machines for a while, I worried. I was concerned she wouldn't feed and hardly moved. My prayers were answered though and she improved every day.

Later when she was a sturdy toddler, chewing almost everything and crashing into, or falling over, everything else I fretted.

"Don't panic, she's growing and learning," Sharon assured me.

Of course we kept things like bleach and knives well away from her reach, but I wasn't allowed to attach foam to every item of furniture. Not that I wanted to. Not really.

By the time Fennel started school my anxieties were mostly under control. She knew not to talk to strangers and her teachers seemed excellent and sensible. I even liked her friends. Other dads moaned about being a taxi service, not me. Providing transport allowed me to see where she went and that she got home safely.

She made Sharon and me proud so many times; when she joined the Girl Guides and got all those badges, her sporting achievements, and the way she helped care for her grandmother. She truly looked like an angel in her white dress at her confirmation and sang like one too both in church and at home. Fennel got straight As in her exams.

Little things still bothered me. Her obsession with the Twilight books and films, the shortness of her skirts and horribleness of every boy she ever dated. She was happy and healthy though. Those things were what really mattered.

Then she got a job away from home. Her dream job, working for a fashion magazine. I was happy for her, but missed her company. Sharon was the worrier then.

"She's getting thin," Sharon said.

"A little slimmer, yes. I expect she's missing your lovely cooking."

"And she looks pale."

"Slightly less tanned I agree, but she's working now and has to spend all day indoors."

"We don't see enough of her."

About that we were in total agreement.

Not long afterwards Fennel was discovered, unconscious, in a seldom visited corner of a churchyard. She was bleeding from a small wound in her neck. It was sheer chance she was found before it was too late. By the time we heard about it she'd been stitched up and started on transfusions.

She didn't look so different from the very first time I'd seen her in an incubator, with machinery keeping her alive. True she was bigger, in a bed and had hair, but she looked just as fragile.

Sharon and I reminded each other she'd always been a fighter. Again our prayers were answered. She was out of hospital in a few days, back at work the following week. Now, with her hair down, there's nothing to show what happened.

Nothing but Jacob. It was him who found her. Sharon was grateful. I was suspicious. Why was he in a graveyard at dawn? Why was she? Though nothing was missing but her phone, the police assumed she'd been mugged. Fennel couldn't remember what happened. I couldn't help speculating.

The more I learned about Jacob, the less I liked him. We invited him to church with us and to stay for Sunday lunch. He was always too busy. Since coming under his influence, Fennel rarely attended services with us either. From things our daughter mentioned it seemed an alarming number of people Jacob came into contact with died shortly afterwards and he was often called into work unexpectedly, sometimes in the middle of the night.

What can a father do though? I welcomed him into my home. Attempted to look pleased when he presented Sharon with enough flowers to cover a coffin and handed me a bottle of blood red wine.

Deliberately I sharpened the silver carving knife as the others made small talk.

"Perhaps you'd like to say grace, Jacob?" I suggested.

He sounded amused as he accepted. He spoke confidently and clearly, as though he'd been practising. It's easy to say what you don't mean. I should know, hadn't I said it was nice to see him?

"How do you like your meat, Jacob? Rare?"

"Yes please." He licked his lips as he watched me carve.

"It's no good, I can't wait any longer," Fennel said. "Mum, Dad, Jacob has asked me to marry him!"

My hand slipped and I nicked my wrist with the sharp blade.

At the sight of the blood Jacob leapt at me. He grabbed my hand and pulled it up towards him in a vice-like grip.

Could my daughter really love a vampire? I felt faint.

It wasn't until Fennel had cleaned the cut and bandaged me up I realised he'd been elevating the injury and applying pressure to stop me losing blood rather than wanting it to flow.

My wife and daughter fussed around me and soon I felt more embarrassed than ill. Jacob stood back, looking concerned and uncomfortable.

"Don't worry, lad. I won't be needing the last rites just yet."

"Just as well. That's a Catholic thing. Like you, I'm an Anglican."

An Anglican vicar actually. One who visits the sick and dying to offer what comfort he can, even if it drags him out into the night. A good man. One almost worthy of my daughter's love.

17. All Talk

"We need to find Cara a nice man," Amy whispered at the dress fitting.

"We've been trying for years, what makes you think we can do it now?" I asked.

"She's seen how happy we both are and I think she's ready to settle down."

Cara swished back the curtain. "What do you think, Lucy?"

"You look beautiful, but I knew you would," I told her. It was true, she'd been a beautiful bridesmaid at Amy's wedding and would do the same for me next month. We'd made a pact to be bridesmaids at each other's weddings. Technically Amy will be my matron of honour, but you don't think of things like that when you're nine.

"What's the matter, Cara?" Amy asked.

"I was just thinking I'm always the bridesmaid… Come on, let's get out of this lot and go for a drink." She went back into the changing room.

"See what I mean?" Amy whispered.

"OK, we'll both try to find someone," I promised.

Over the next few days, whenever I wasn't fretting about my reception seating plan, I considered every single man I met as a potential partner for Cara. It was bizarre; as teenagers we were sure Cara would be the first to get married. It hadn't worked out like that. Maybe our slightly jealous teasing was part of the trouble. Amy and I used to spend ages putting on make-up and choosing flattering clothes, yet never looked half as good as Cara.

"It's all right for you," I'd moaned. "You're so pretty you don't have to make any effort."

"She's right," Amy agreed. "Us two might as well turn up an hour after you, because it takes that long for the boys to even notice we're there, they're that busy staring at you."

"What good are blokes like that, though?" Cara had asked. "I don't want someone who only sees what I'm like on the outside and will dump me for someone younger and prettier the moment I get a grey hair or wrinkle."

We could almost see her point. Amy is quite pretty, but her sense of fun is her main attraction. She and her husband are always laughing and joking, I'm sure they'll be happy no matter how much their appearances change. I'm no oil painting but I've got a wonderful fiancé who loves every plain, cuddly inch of me – and there are a lot of inches!

Cara got kind of crazy about it. If a bloke told her too many times she looked good then she'd dump him.

"You're being daft," I told her.

"Just because a bloke pays you a compliment doesn't mean he can't see past the way you look," Amy agreed.

Cara decided to educate herself so she had more than a pretty face and good figure to attract a man. The idea was OK in theory. We imagined she'd watch Top Gear or study football scores. We were wrong. Whenever a man started chatting her up, Cara blurted out bizarre facts and looked a complete nutter.

I was thinking about Cara's weird way of talking as I ate my green salad at work.

"There's not enough protein in that," a deep voice informed me.

I tried to explain about my wedding dress being a bit tighter than I'd like, but he wittered on about amino acids and vitamin B.

"No good chatting her up, Jamie," one of my colleagues called over. "She's engaged."

Jamie blushed. "Sorry, I wasn't… er …"

"No harm done," I said. "My name's Lucy, I gather yours is Jamie?"

We shook hands.

"I hope you don't mind me talking to you? I'm not good with girls and you looked approachable …"

Perhaps Cara's beauty scared men off even before her weird conversations did? Jamie might be different. He was on the skinny side, but otherwise presentable and he seemed to be looking for female companionship.

"Do you fancy meeting me in the pub one evening? I have some nice girlfriends you can practice chatting too," I offered.

The evening started well. When Jamie's comment on the weather was met by Cara's description of cumulus nimbus clouds, he replied with something about isobars.

Then I made the mistake of mentioning food. I guessed correctly that Jamie would give his proteins and acids chatter and that she'd respond with the merits of various cuts of meat. Cara's Uncle is a butcher and he'd been pleased to share his knowledge with her. What I didn't know was that Jamie was a vegetarian. The fervent, preachy kind. The rest of the evening didn't go well.

Amy rang a couple of days later. "I think I've found a man

for Cara. His name's Sam. I met him in the dentist and he started talking about spiritual enlightenment and fate."

"That's great. Cara's always looking up people's horoscopes, they should have lots to talk about."

That evening didn't even start well. Sam was a devout Christian and approved of neither Cara's attitude to spiritualism nor to the spirits in our glasses. After he'd left, Cara made us promise not to arrange any more blind dates.

"Can we go somewhere else next week? Just the three of us. We could consider it a training session for your hen night, Lucy."

We met at the pub she'd suggested. It was heaving!

"Sorry, girls. I've only been here once before. It was really quiet then. Let's go somewhere else," Cara said. "We'll never get a seat and we can't talk properly."

"Let's have one as we're here. Maybe it'll get quieter later?" I said.

"It's always busy here on Tuesdays, girls," a man told us. "You can share my table if you like. I was expecting someone, but I've just had a text to say they can't come."

"Thanks," Amy and I said together. We sat before Cara could say no.

She shrugged. "OK. I'll get the drinks. Usual for you two?"

We nodded.

"Can I get you one?" she asked the man.

"Thanks, but I'm fine," he said indicating a half full beer glass.

He was about our age, I noted and quite attractive. Friendly too.

"I hope your girlfriend isn't ill?" Amy asked.

"I don't have a girlfriend," he told us. As he explained the friend he'd been waiting for had car trouble, I caught Amy's look. We were both thinking the same thing.

"Nice pub this," Cara said as she returned with the drinks. "I got served right away even though they're busy."

"I'm not surprised," our new friend said.

"Oh, why's that?" Cara asked.

I held my breath. Amy looked as though she was doing the same. If this bloke said it was because of her looks he might regret offering to share the table.

"Landlord likes to make newcomers welcome. I'm Dave, by the way."

"I'm pleased to meet you, Dave," Cara said and gave him our names.

Dave fiddled with the vase of flowers on the table.

"Pretty carnations," Cara said. She's very fond of flowers.

"Is that what they are? I don't know anything about flowers."

Amy and I tried to start a conversation about the weather.

"Shame the rain stopped the tennis," Dave said. "Have you girls been following the matches at Wimbledon?"

"No," Cara said. "I prefer horse racing."

Dave didn't know anything about horse racing.

"The food looks good," I said, hoping to bring the conversation round to something we could all talk about.

"It does, doesn't it?" Cara said. "They've got halibut; that's my favourite fish."

Dave hadn't been positive halibut was a fish. "I'm more of

a steak and chips man."

Cara told him the names of every single cut of steak and a whole list of potato varieties that made good chips. He looked kind of surprised.

"You do know some unusual facts," he said.

"That's nothing. I can tell you the source of ..."

I interrupted, hoping to stop her before things got awkward. "We've finished our drinks, perhaps it's time to go?"

"We might as well stay, now we're here," Cara said.

"Please stay," Dave pleaded. "It's my round ..."

"OK," Amy agreed. "It's my round though. Lucy, will you help me carry them?"

Amy and I didn't get served straight away, but the pub was even busier than when Cara had gone to the bar. We kept an eye on Cara. She was doing a lot of talking and judging from the way she was moving her hands, some of it was about spider's webs.

"So why is it so busy here on Tuesdays?" Amy asked when we got back with the drinks.

"It's quiz night. Will you ladies be on my team?"

Between them, Dave and Cara answered every question. After collecting the prize of a bottle of wine, and sharing it with us, Dave asked Cara one further question.

"Will you join me here when the pub is quieter, so we can both try the halibut?"

Cara gave the answer we all wanted to hear. I was delighted right up until the moment I realised I'd have to redo the seating plan for my reception.

18. Diamond Disaster

"I've been thinking about our sixtieth anniversary, love," Judie said.

"Me too. I want to make it really special, make up for the times things haven't always gone to plan."

She squeezed Will's hand. "You don't need to do that. Actually I thought it would be nice just to have a lazy day at home with no pressure. Invite the family round and just buy in the food. Something like that?"

"If you're sure that's what you really want?" Will said.

It wasn't, but it seemed safer to Judie than the alternative. Staying at home would be an anticlimax compared to some of the things they'd done, or tried to do, on previous anniversaries but in truth their romantic trips away had never gone well.

For their honeymoon they'd borrowed a caravan. They'd got lost and ended up in the staff car park of a sewage treatment plant. Luckily the wind had been in the right direction, it was quite late by the time they'd parked and it was their wedding night so the view hadn't bothered them.

When they arrived for their first ever foreign holiday, the hotel hadn't actually been built and they ended up in a tent on the beach. That wasn't Will's fault of course. He was responsible for the time they'd spent their anniversary in a maternity ward – but no more than she was. She did blame him a bit for the time he lost his credit card and they had to stay in a hostel for the homeless on one trip.

Judie wouldn't change those memories for anything. Each disaster had been an adventure, brought them closer together and passed into family legend, but she was older now. Not just older, actually old she admitted. She needed her home comforts, she couldn't sleep on the floor or she'd not get up and neither would Will. They were still sound in mind and body, but for how much longer?

She'd love a night or two somewhere fancy being pampered, but it probably wouldn't happen and she couldn't take the disappointment. Not hers, she'd found it all hilarious and done quite well out of the various disasters, once being put up in a really nice hotel as compensation for a cancelled flight and twice selling their travel stories to a magazine.

It was Will's disappointment she couldn't handle. He always wanted the best for her and nearly always achieved it. He'd arranged lovely birthday parties for her, or trips to the theatre and he'd done the same for the children and grandchildren. It was just their anniversaries that went wrong. Each time he planned more carefully than before and each time it went worse than before. She couldn't bear to see the hurt in his eyes if the trip were to go wrong again.

On their anniversary all of their children and grandchildren arrived as Judie and Will were getting up. They opened cards and presents as a breakfast feast was prepared for them. It was a warm day, so they enjoyed freshly squeezed orange juice, smoked salmon and scrambled eggs, pancakes with luscious ripe berries and pots of fragrant coffee, in the garden. The meal lasted a long time and was punctuated by friends and neighbours popping in with gifts and good wishes.

"How odd that everyone has come this morning," Judie

remarked. It had been a glorious few hours, but wouldn't the rest of the day seem a little flat?

"I thought it best as we shan't be here this afternoon," Will said. "I'm taking you away, my dear."

"Oh!" She didn't know whether to be pleased or concerned.

"Don't worry, Mum. I've programmed the sat nav," their son said.

"And we've checked both your mobiles are working and we'll all have our phones on if you need rescuing," said their youngest daughter.

"And Dad has cash in case his card won't work," their eldest said.

"The car has been serviced and fuelled," a neighbour promised.

It seemed that everything had been taken care of, but Judie knew better. Once out of sight of their waving family she made Will pull over and told him how much she loved him, how wonderful the morning had been and how it really wouldn't matter if the trip was a disaster.

"It's the thought that counts?" he suggested.

"Yes, love. So where are we going?"

"Well I thought about what you said before, about the disasters always being OK in the end …"

Maybe he was going to take her home again just as she'd suggested? That would be a shame because she was now looking forward to going away.

"So I thought we'd go back to where it all started."

They'd met on a youth club trip. "Surely you're not thinking of driving to Wales?

"No, I meant when our disastrous trips first started."

"Our honeymoon? You're taking me to a sewage works?"

"Yes, love."

She'd spoken too soon about him still having all his faculties!

"It's logical. If I plan a disastrous trip then it's bound to work out all right."

Judie laughed. "You've planned a disaster? That's a first."

They drove in silence for a few minutes. She supposed he was just taking her for a drive, possibly to be followed by a nice dinner if she was lucky. She'd enjoy that.

He asked if she recognised anything.

"No, I expect everything has changed."

"Oh dear, it looks like you're right," he said as he stopped the car.

As she looked where he was pointing she did indeed recognise the elaborate Victorian facade to the sewage plant, or rather what used to be the sewage plant. It had since been turned into a luxury spa hotel.

Two uniformed young men asked, "Mr and Mrs Jones?"

Will nodded.

"Welcome to Freshwater spa. Your suite is ready for you. My colleague will park your car, may I take your bags?"

"This is no disaster, Will!"

"True. Looks like I messed up again then," Will said as they followed the smart young man down a plushly carpeted hallway and into a room where flowers, a huge balloon with 'Happy 6oth' on and bottle of champagne awaited them.

"It does, but I think I can find it in my heart to forgive you just once more."

19. Just Two Months

Jane thought the planned barbecue was rapidly turning into a baby shower. When her son and his wife had first suggested it, there were only going to be a few of them sharing sausages and a couple of French sticks. Still she supposed that with her first grandchild due in just two month's time, they'd all be focussing on that anyway.

May, usually a slim, pale little thing, was absolutely glowing. Jane had to fight the urge to keep patting her daughter-in-law's very obvious bump.

"May's parents are staying with us for a few days. We thought you might like to see your fellow grandparents-to-be," her son had said.

"I would, thank you." May's parents didn't live close by, so other than one birthday party, the wedding, and a Christmas lunch, Jane hadn't really spent any time with them. They were both very nice though and she'd got on well with them on those previous occasions, especially May's mother who was also called Jane. They'd make very different grandparents she thought. This Jane wouldn't be able to assist financially, but could call round to babysit at very short notice and help with practical matters. May's parents would be glamorous occasional visitors who'd swoop in, shower the child with gifts and affection then vanish again. They'd have novelty value, but Jane would get more cuddles.

Demonstrating her practicality, Jane said. "Can I bring

anything?"

"If you've got any salad to spare, you could bring a handful of leaves."

"No problem. I have masses growing."

"In that case, could I take some rocket home?" May asked. "I want to eat spicy food all the time at the moment. I'm not sure it's good to have too much, but salad can't do any harm, can it?"

"I'll pick you some with pleasure. I don't think you need worry what you eat though. I craved chilli con carne during my pregnancy and it didn't do my little boy any harm."

May had glanced at her six foot four husband and said, "It didn't stunt his growth at any rate."

Jane's little boy had phoned her the following day. "If you meant it about having masses of salad, then please bring it to the barbecue. We thought we should invite the neighbours and somehow ended up including the whole street, May's brother and his family and some of our friends."

"I'd be delighted." Jane was pleased to be able to help and happy her carefully nurtured lettuce, radish and oriental vegetables wouldn't go to waste. "And I'll make sure I include plenty more rocket."

"Thanks. May's already eaten the lot you gave her yesterday."

Jane grinned as she thought of the bulging carrier bag she'd given her. What really made her smile though was the easy way her son had asked for the favour. Ever since, aged about eight, he'd first got teased about the name she'd given him she'd felt there was a little reserve in the way he treated her. Jane didn't think that was fair.

From the minute Jane suspected she was pregnant, she

was determined to give her baby a more interesting name than her own. At school she'd been one of six girls with the same name and most of the other girls had Jane as a middle name. When she was told to expect a girl born close to Christmas day she'd put her imagination to work. Noël sounded so pretty said the French way, but people might pronounce it Noel which wouldn't be right for the child she already thought of as her Christmas angel. Holly was rather nice, as was Christina. Ivy she discounted as it had been the name of an elderly and rather unpleasant neighbour when she was a child. Carol or Mary were appropriate as would Eve be if the girl was born on the twenty-fourth.

As it was, she had a son on the seventeenth. He had rather a red nose and she briefly considered naming him Rudolph, but she'd looked down at her surprisingly sturdy, dark haired boy and changed her mind. His wrinkled face had looked so serious, she felt he deserved a name to match. Besides he wasn't really a Christmas baby at all. She named him December.

All had been well until his classmates decided it wasn't a proper name.

"Why did you call me that, Mummy? It's stupid."

After she explained she said, "So you see I had to choose something else quickly and I was right, it does suit you."

He'd burst out, "But it's not really a name."

"It is now. It's your name."

"It's not. Everyone says so."

"Sorry, love." She'd long since given up arguing with an eight-year-old against the power of 'everyone'.

"Is my middle name a real one?"

"Yes. It was passed down through your father's family."

"I'll use that then."

"I wouldn't, love. I had no idea December would get you teased, but I'm pretty sure Algernon will."

"Really? That's just great."

"Sorry, love."

For a while he'd called himself, Dec. That wasn't really successful. The boys who'd teased him called him Decs and said he was named after Christmas decorations. By the time Ant and Dec became popular TV stars, December was already over six feet and very unlike those cheeky chappies in personality. The comparison made him seem dour, which he wasn't really. He'd gone back to his full name, which pleased Jane even though she'd felt he might never really forgive her for giving it to him.

Then a few years ago, some friends of his organised a joint party for him and someone else who had the same birthday. He'd come home, not entirely sober, to discover Jane was waiting up for him.

"Thash show shweet, Mum."

"Well, you're still my little boy, December," she'd said as she reached up to smooth his very ruffled hair. He was too, despite being over a foot taller and almost twice her bodyweight.

"Your little Deshember." He'd grinned as he slurred it. "Did I already have the name by thish time on the day I wash born?"

"It's now the day after your birthday and yes, you did. You were born about lunchtime and I'd decided on your name before the nurse brought me a cup of tea that afternoon."

He'd kissed her before going to bed. Not a dutiful peck, but had pulled her into a hug and planted a smacker on each cheek.

From then on that touch of reserve, she'd thought he'd previously displayed towards her, had gone. Jane guessed he'd met a pretty girl at the party who'd told him it was a nice name. It was almost two years later she discovered the truth. By then December was living away from home and in a serious relationship with May. Her name together with her delicate appearance put Jane in mind of a silvery mayfly flitting from flower to flower. Jane had liked the pretty, lively and cheerful girl from the start, so when December asked if he could bring May for a birthday tea she hadn't hesitated.

"What would you like? A proper grown up meal, or a big cake and jelly and ice cream?"

"The jelly and ice cream bit, I think. May's never really had that kind of birthday party."

"Never?"

"No, with her birthday being when it is, hers always felt like Christmas parties, she says."

Jane had always been very careful to see that didn't happen with December's birthdays. She knew May's family had moved around a lot though, because of her father's job. That had probably made organising separate parties difficult, but …

"When is May's birthday, love?"

"I thought you knew? It's the same as mine."

"Oh! But …"

"Apparently she was named after her Mum's best friend, who'd helped her through the pregnancy and birth because her dad was away."

"Oh I see. And you met her at a party for both of you two

years ago? Well jelly and ice cream it is, plus two huge cakes I think."

"In that case, can I invite the people who got us together and make a real party of it?"

That party had expanded she recalled. May's parents had called the day before and announced they were making a flying visit, literally, to see her. Naturally they had been included, as had May's brother. It had been a success.

Jane knew the barbecue turned baby shower would be too. Determined to do her bit to help, as well as preparing salads, she offered to make a cake.

"That'd be great, Mum but it'll need to be massive to feed everyone," December said.

"I'll make two then, it wouldn't be the first time."

It seemed fitting, when the time came to bring out the cakes, to ask the other Jane, May's mum, to help her. The two women chatted together like old friends as they removed the film from the cakes and lifted them carefully onto trays.

"These are brilliant, Jane. You're going to be in demand for birthday cakes for our grandchild I know."

"And he or she will love the things you give them too, Jane. You have a real knack for finding interesting gifts. Everyone who sees that cute little reindeer you gave me asks where I got it."

"Thank you. You know I reckon between us we have this grandmother thing covered."

"Except for what the child will call us. If we're both Granny that will be confusing and it seems silly for one of us to be Granny Jane."

"Yes. We should sort that out. May's been threatening to

call me Gummy, or Ne-naw, ne-naw, in revenge for the name I gave her."

"She doesn't like it? But it's so pretty and really suits her."

"Just as December's suits him."

"Hmmm, see what you mean. Shall we toss for Granny and the other be Nanna?"

"If you prefer Granny you can have that. My own grandmother was known as Noni and I'd rather like to use that."

"Deal." They solemnly shook on it.

There was a lot of laughter as they carried out the cakes which died into silence as they approached.

"What's going on?" they both demanded.

May's brother explained. "It's about that baby name book. You know you were both asked to tick all the names you like?"

"Yes."

The women looked at each other. Jane felt they were both acknowledging the fact they'd been surprised to be asked.

"It's so they can choose from whichever are left," a giggling guest informed them.

Laughter broke out again.

"This will be remembered when you want a babysitter," Jane said, trying not to smile.

"Yes, and you can forget that cheque I promised for fitting out the nursery," May's mum added, even less convincingly.

"Oh dear, now you've done it," May said in mock concern. "You'd better tell them, December."

"We've already picked a nice sensible name for our daughter."

The two grannys-to-be, and everyone else, oohed and ahhed at the news the baby due in two month's time was a girl.

"What is it?" both Janes demanded.

"We're not going to tell you," December said.

"Not even a tiny clue?"

"Yes, OK," May said. "We're going to name her after one of her grandmothers."

20. Trying To Be Nice

I missed the train by seconds. The guard saw me though, I swear he did. Looked through me like I were a ghost. Would he stop the train? Oh no. The schedule's far more important than the needs of a customer. Doesn't matter that I might have had something important to do.

That's how things are at present. Nothing works out for me. Even actual presents. Gave one to Joanna for Valentine's, but she gave it back.

"It's not appropriate, Darryl."

"What's not appropriate about a nice gold chain with my name on it?"

She never did answer me. That was last month, I should try to let it go, I tell myself just as me mum told me.

Right in front of me are some of those stupid posters. You know, the ones about the trains shutting the doors just before departing and how the rubbish staff have the right to be respected. Next to them's the timetable. It's like they're laughing at people who've missed their train.

I just stop myself punching the vending machine. Joanna wouldn't like it. She wants people to be nice and kind. All the time. To everyone. She'd say I should stop and consider those who might want to use it.

Can't think why, but she's the girl I want. Can't think why, but she doesn't want me. I'm a good looking bloke. Plenty of girls fancy me, it's just her who has to be difficult. Never had any trouble with women before. Relationships didn't last long, but then I didn't want them too.

Joanna lent me a book to read. "It might help you to understand."

I didn't like that much. It's not as though I'm stupid. Pretty quick on the uptake I am – unlike that drip Eddie who's always hanging around her. Ought to tell him to push off, but she's too nice to do it.

Joanna is always telling me to look on the bright side. She seems to think there always is one. The bright side of her giving me the book was that I'd have to return it. Clearly she did want to see me again, despite what she'd said.

I got through, 'A Christmas Carol' as quick as I could. When I'd finished, I went straight round to hers and made it clear I was happy to pay for dinner. She explained that's not why she'd said no.

"It's not about money."

"Right. Yeah, the book did seem to say that," I admitted.

"Did you read every page?"

I'd skimmed through looking for some laughs. There hadn't been many. I took it back again, saying I'd read it more carefully.

"Start right at the beginning," she advised.

It's cold and draughty on the platform and there's naff all to do, so I'm stuck in the train station waiting room with the book and a grubby old man. I don't want to talk to him. He looks hard work. I start to read, but then I start to think. Is he the ghost of Christmas future? Will I be all sad and alone like him one day? Joanna would want me to be nice. Maybe it won't hurt me to try.

"Good book this," I hold it up so he can see the cover.

He nods. Doesn't look up.

"Christmas Carol."

He mumbles about Dickens, who is the author in case you didn't know, but doesn't seem interested.

"Fancy a coffee?"

"No thank you," he says.

"I'd pay," I assure him.

"No."

Not letting his rudeness put me off, I try again to make conversation.

He looks up. "Young man, as I said, I'm trying to write an article on double-digging."

That's when I spot his notebook. I never listen, Joanna said, don't pay attention to others. Maybe she's right.

I pull out my mobile. The old bloke sighs. Taking the hint, I go outside to make my call. This time, I let Joanna do the talking.

She says she still doesn't think I understand.

"I do. I get it now. I gotta listen and pay attention."

"Did you listen to what I said about the book?"

"Yeah, yeah, start at the beginning." I flip open the cover so I can read her the boring bit about copyright to prove my point. That's when I see it, written in biro.

'*To my darling Joanna, from your Eddie. x x x*'

"So it's serious with you two?" I ask, just to be sure I really have got it this time.

"We're getting married."

There's nothing nice I can say to that, so I hang up. There's a reason I don't listen; when I do, I hear stuff like that. Joanna doesn't want to go out with me, or Dad isn't going to live with us anymore, or I can't get a job without qualifications and have to go back to college.

I go back into the waiting room. I don't slam the door. It isn't the kind you can slam. The old bloke doesn't notice my misery, don't think he even realises I've come back. He's got his own troubles apparently as he's scribbling furiously. I stare for a bit before sussing his pen's run out and chuck him mine. He notices that.

"Oh! Thank you, young man. That's very kind of you."

I shrug. It's just a pen.

A train arrives. Not mine. An old woman gets off. Older even than the bloke doing his writing. Someone hands down a big case and it looks like she's thanking them. The train goes and the woman is still there. She tries lifting the case, but nothing happens. Then she tries pulling it, but that's not a whole lot better. She's starting to get on my nerves so I go out.

"Where d'you want it?"

"Oh thank you. It's too heavy for me and my grand daughter is …"

"Where d'you want it?" I try again before she gives me her life history.

"Just out the front, if you'd be so kind."

I pick it up and she follows me.

"Here OK?"

She says it is. Just as well because I've spotted Milly from college. She's well fit and I don't want her seeing me doing anything soppy like carrying old lady's bags. The silly old bat doesn't get it though and grabs hold of me saying how kind I am and how grateful she is.

Daft old bat spots Milly, but that's no help.

"Milly darling," she says and they hug each other. "This nice young man carried my bag for me, wasn't that kind of him?"

"Yes, Nan it was. Thanks, Darryl." She flashes me a smile that makes me want to join in the hugging.

"Oh, you two know each other?"

"We're at college together." Milly introduces me.

Nan rambles on about it being nice for Milly to have such a kind friend.

"I'd better go, my train will be here in a minute," I say. I can't miss this one, Mum needs me back to babysit my kid sister while she does her cleaning job. "See you Monday, Milly."

"I'll look forward to it." She flashes that smile again.

This time, I catch the train. Once I've got a seat I ring Mum to let her know I'm on my way. Then I ring Joanna.

"Congratulations on your engagement. I hope you and Eddie will be very happy together," I say.

I'm not sure I mean it, but I'm trying to be nice. Joanna seems pleased. Surprised, but pleased. The weirdest thing is, I sort of feel nice as she thanks me for my good wishes and says she hopes I too, will find someone I can be happy with.

21. Life's Little Sacrifices

Helen waved goodbye to Tracie and pressed the button to close the car window. There was a squeal as it slid up and then stopped about half an inch from the top. She tried opening and closing it again. The screech it gave as it moved was louder, but the gap remained. She couldn't see anything obviously wrong, so drove home with an icy blast down her neck.

When Robert got home that evening, he had no more luck solving the problem. "You'll have to book it into the garage," he told her.

"OK, I'll give them a call."

"Quite a common problem with that model, but easy enough to fix," the mechanic assured her. "We're really busy at the moment, but leave it with us and we'll get to it as soon as we can."

It seemed her independence would have to be temporarily sacrificed for her more long term comfort. The ever practical Pete could probably have fixed it straight away, but she couldn't very well ask him. Instead she arranged to leave it at the garage the following day, then told Robert what they'd said.

"So, I'll need you to pick me up from the garage and drop me at work on Thursday, then take me in to collect it when they're done. Oh actually that's my book group night, so I'll need a lift there too."

"What? That's too much faffing about. Ring the garage and cancel. You can always turn the heater on if it's cold."

"But it'll have to be done sometime. If rain gets in it'll …"

"Yes, yes, but do it on a day you're not working and stay in town or something until it's done."

"But …"

"Sit down a minute, I want to talk to you."

She sat and was presented with estate agent's details for a house. Rather a nice looking house with a large well laid out garden and three bathrooms.

"What do you think?" Robert asked.

"You want to move? Again?"

They'd moved several times since they married and each time she, and the children, had made the sacrifice for his career. She'd never spoken against his plans except when they'd have meant moving the children at particularly difficult times school-wise. Even then all she'd asked was that they wait until their daughter started secondary school or their son had taken his exams.

Helen always hated the upheaval and that the family had to make, and then lose, friends each time. That never bothered Robert. He didn't seem interested in anything much apart from work and his model planes. While she unpacked precious possessions, helped the children adjust to a new school and filled in endless change of address forms, he'd be shut away gluing plastic pieces together. She'd thought downsizing when the children moved out, so he had the money to set up in business for himself, was the last time she'd have to go through all that.

"We can afford somewhere bigger now," Robert said.

"This house is plenty big enough for the two of us." At

least it had been when they'd moved in. What should have been a spare bedroom and dining room were both filled with his models. Not just the models, but also the boxes the pieces came in and every unused sticker, spare part and dried up pot of paint just in case they ever came in useful for another project.

She didn't really mind his hobby, though she couldn't help wishing that if it couldn't be something tidy it would at least be useful, like Pete's was.

Robert read out the dimensions of key rooms and details of how conveniently placed the house was for the motorway and train station.

Helen said, "I'm settled here. I have friends, a job I enjoy and there's the book club."

She thought he'd accepted her point of view until she arrived home, cold and irritable from the draughty window, to find an estate agent waiting to measure up the house.

Robert was home in time to hear him say, "It's a nice property, but would be improved by clearing out the clutter and repainting it in neutral colours."

Although Helen had been saying the same for years with no result, Robert decided to take the young man's advice. He immediately arranged to take time off work and within a week they'd tidied, redecorated, and disposed of all but a few of his better model planes. Helen admitted the ones he'd kept looked quite good. Displayed hanging in the dining room, against newly painted pale blue walls, they suggested sky and almost added to the spacious feeling created by the lack of clutter. Sacrificing their free time to decorate was a small price to pay for the finished result, or would have been if they'd get to enjoy it.

"You see, there's plenty of space here," Helen said. "We

don't need to move."

"It's already on the market," Robert said, "We might as well see what offers we get."

It sounded as though he might be having second thoughts.

"This is a really nice area, Robert. Friendly neighbours and shops and the park nearby …"

"Very true. That should help us get the asking price."

"And everywhere we want to go is so accessible. I wouldn't want to have to drive down the motorway in my old car just to get a pint of milk or for the book club."

"You won't have to. I was going to keep it a surprise, but I can't really… I'm buying you a better car."

"It would be nice to have one with windows which close."

"Hmm, that's why I couldn't make it a surprise. We're trading in your old one, but we have to get the window fixed first. You drop it at the garage tomorrow and I'll pick you up."

"And you'll have to take me in the next day."

"Yes, which is Thursday so you'll need a lift to book club."

Why couldn't he have just done that when she first asked, not waited until she'd driven round in icy misery for weeks?

"Don't put yourself out!" she snapped. "I'll go to Tracie's after work and we can go together. Just pick me up afterwards."

There was two hours to fill between finishing work and going to book club, maybe she'd manage an uninterrupted hour with Pete? Thanks to all the decorating she'd barely had time to think about him this last week, let alone get her hands on him.

"Yes, of course you can come back to mine," Tracie said. "Or I can drop you home if you want to eat with Robert before book club."

"I don't, thanks. Let him get his own tea for once, that tiny sacrifice will be the only one he makes in this whole sorry mess."

"Want to talk about it?"

"No, I want it not to be happening." She did talk though, as soon as they left work.

"I'm furious, Tracie. Robert wants us to move and hasn't listened to me when I've tried to say I don't. For years I've been the one making sacrifices to help his career and raise his children."

"And he hasn't even noticed?" Tracie guessed.

"No, I don't think he has. I didn't use to begrudge it, but this is the final straw. He wouldn't sort out the rubbish from his models so I had a pleasant home to live in, but one word from the estate agent sent him into action. It was too much trouble to give me a lift to the garage and save me the discomfort of chilly drives and a stiff neck, but he was quite happy to do it for the stranger who'll next own the car."

Tracie didn't say a word, just drove her friend home and made her a cup of tea.

"Sorry to moan," Helen said. "I feel better now I've got all that off my chest. Robert's not all bad really."

"Nah, he's all right." Tracie broke into a grin. "Maybe you're just comparing him unfavourably with Pete?"

"Probably. And that's hardly fair, is it? Robert probably thinks he's doing what's best."

"Sounds to me like he doesn't appreciate what he's got until he's about to lose it."

"True," Helen said.

"Unlike me. I appreciate having you as a friend and a work colleague and I'm not going to wait until I've lost you to do something about it."

"You have a plan?"

"Two actually. The first one is…. As you don't have to drive tonight, we should treat ourselves to a Chinese take away and a bottle of wine?"

"Your plans are good!" Helen said. She was even more impressed after hearing the second one.

Robert was waiting for her outside the pub after book club. When they got home she saw he'd loaded the dishwasher after cooking his own meal. That had been pasta in tomato sauce if the splatters around the cooker were anything to go by.

Helen made him a coffee and took it into the dining room where he was repainting a Sopwith Camel biplane. She didn't quite shut the door after her. The phone rang a few minutes later. It was Tracie calling.

"Yes, I'm fine," Helen said. "Nothing like a couple of hours of good company to cheer me up if you know what I mean."

"You'll have to speak up. Now tell me about Pete."

Loudly, Helen did that, saying how charming Pete was, how good looking, how practical. "He's so much more considerate than Robert too. You know nothing has actually happened between us, but sometimes I really think I could be persuaded."

"Would you want a permanent relationship?" Tracie asked.

"Leave Robert you mean? I don't really want to, but if I'm

going to have all the upheaval of moving whatever I do, then it's something to consider. Oh, hold on a minute ..." Helen pulled the door tight shut before finishing the conversation.

As they got ready for bed that night, Robert said, "I've been thinking… perhaps moving house isn't such a good idea?"

"Oh? Has something made you change your mind?"

"Yes, what you were saying. You're right, this place is big enough for us and it's a nice area. I realise you have your job and you've made friends here. Maybe I should settle down and do the same?"

"I'd like that, Robert. And if we're staying, maybe the book group could meet here? The pub is a bit noisy and all sorts of people come and join in. Some are very charming and everything, but it's a bit distracting."

"That's an excellent idea. Yes, the book club would be most welcome."

So that Robert wouldn't be inconvenienced by the meeting, Helen re arranged the furniture as soon as she finished work, leaving Robert one chair in the dining room so he could work on his models. The rest went into the living room before she cooked Robert's favourite supper.

To her surprise, Robert didn't immediately disappear, but welcomed her friends and fussed over seats and cushions until everyone was comfortable. Then said, "I'll come back in an hour to see if you're ready for tea."

The group had an animated discussion about the book they'd just finished reading. The author's skill at creating a fascinating plot, interesting location and characters they'd cared about was widely dissected and praised over the next two hours. Helen wasn't the only one to confess herself halfway in love with the handsome, charming and practically minded hero.

Robert got engrossed in his aerial world and didn't arrive with the promised tea until the book group were discussing what they'd read next. None of them, except perhaps Helen and Tracie, realised that meant he'd sacrificed the peace of mind he'd have got from learning Pete was no more than words on a page brought to life in the reader's imagination.

22. Finishing The Sequence

I'm sitting in the sunshine picking petals off a daisy.

"He loves me, he loves me not."

I know it's a daft thing to do. I know it won't tell me how Martin feels. Random chance decides which answer comes up last. Odd even, loves me, loves me not, round and round in sequence until there's nothing left but the certainty that you have destroyed something beautiful and still don't know.

It's all about sequences, my life. The green, amber, red of the traffic light which meant I stopped at the junction. The salt lick, lime squeeze, tequila shot after tequila shot for the guy in the van which meant he didn't. No doubt a sequence of events led to his uncontrolled drinking. Something small, then something else and it spiralled out of control. He is sorry. I know because he told me.

Sorry doesn't help me get out of bed in the mornings. Someone had to do that for me until a few days ago. I've worked on my physio, had grab handles put in, learnt the techniques. Now I'm able to wrestle on clothes and lug myself into the chair. Today I wheeled myself into the garden for the first time. One day perhaps I'll be able to take a shower unaided, get myself onto a bus, maybe even find a job. These are goals for me to reach for, one after the other. They're the ones I dare to contemplate.

I've been going through the circle of grief, the psychologist says. Another sequence. Shock, denial, anger and guilt, despair and depression, acceptance. It's not a circle though; it's a spiral. At first the stages were tight. The tiny circle of gold and solitaire diamond that's no longer on my finger. That worried me more than my injuries. Why wasn't I wearing it? It must be a mistake. Was it stolen? Did I lose it?

I was very down about it, but did come to accept the ring was just a symbol. My real fear was that what it represented was gone too. Partially gone: my love for him was as strong as ever and I knew he still felt something for me.

My injuries are something I can live with. Making Martin do the same, by holding him to a promise made when things were different, isn't. When I learned someone in the hospital had removed my ring, and Mum had taken it for safe-keeping, I told her to give it to Martin.

"You're in no state to make a decision like that," she said.

"I'm not making a decision. Just saying he should look after it."

She was right that I couldn't make that decision. I should have told him it's over, set him free, but I didn't. I couldn't.

Martin came to see me every day, but I'm no longer the woman I once was. I wanted to tell him I loved him and hear him declare the same in return. But only if he both said, and meant, it. I wasn't ready for the cruel silence or the kind lie. I'll never be ready for that.

Instead I told him about my memory loss. That I didn't remember the proposal, that we couldn't fulfil our plans, that I was a different person, that our engagement didn't count any more. It wasn't all lies.

When the medication was reduced, my body informed me the empty third finger of my left hand was only part of the bigger picture. It was all about the pain, about me.

Then I went round again and saw how it hurt my parents

and those closest to me: Martin.

Then I saw him, the guy in the van. The circles got wider. Took in the future, outside intensive care, outside hospital, but never outside the chair.

On each loop I learned more – about the treatments available, the equipment to help, the changes in the way others perceived me, and more about my loss. About the walk down the aisle I'll never take, so many things we'd planned to do and now I never could. I was never good at accepting help, being patient, making the best of things. I'm learning.

I've changed. Physically of course. That's a fact I'm beginning to accept even as I'm fighting to get stronger, to earn some independence. I won't stay in bed if I can haul myself out. I won't sit in the shadows if I can manoeuvre myself into the sunshine, just as I have today.

I reach down and pluck a daisy from the lawn. I pull off petals.

"He loves me, he loves me not."

It's a daft thing to do and won't give me answers, so I stop before I've completely destroyed something beautiful.

"Lovely day," Martin says.

I hadn't known he was here, but I don't jump in alarm. He's in my thoughts so much that his presence isn't a shock.

He gestures to the petals. "How far did you get?"

"I stopped at six."

"Loves you not?"

"It doesn't mean anything," I say, willing him to remove another.

He crouches down, but only so he can look into my eyes.

"I've been thinking about what you said. That if you don't remember our engagement then it doesn't count."

My memory isn't the point. It never was.

Martin kneels in front of me. He holds out the same velvet box, open to show the same ring. He asks me the same question with the same mix of love and hope.

Then I get it. I am the same person. I'm damaged, but still me. If that's good enough for him, then it's good enough for me. When I pull another petal from the daisy, to end the sequence on an odd number, on 'he loves me', the ring is on my finger.

23. Hopeless Romantic

The crossword had been tricky, but it hadn't beaten Sydney. "I could do with a cup of tea after that," he said.

"Me too," Levia said.

She didn't make a move. Perhaps she hadn't really heard? She didn't always pay him much attention when she was reading. He didn't get it; why would a woman want that romantic rot when she had her own flesh and blood husband in the room?

Eventually Levia closed her book. "Oh, that was lovely!"

"Don't know why you bother reading those things. Real life isn't like that."

"That's why! For a bit of escapism, a bit of fun." She hauled herself out her chair and abandoned him with, "a girl likes a chance to swoon now and then," as her parting shot.

Maybe she wouldn't have ignored him if he'd offered to do whatever it was the men in those books did, instead of just wanting tea? He'd have to make it himself now.

Levia was in the kitchen. Although the kettle was on she was drinking water.

"That's better, I was gasping, but I wanted to finish the book. I promised to give it back to Jenny this afternoon."

Oh. Maybe he should have made her a cup of tea. Actually she'd hinted as much. Sidney was good at listening to his wife. Unfortunately he was rubbish at acting on what he heard. Or had been.

He had a plan. He'd get the book and carry out some of the romantic stuff. Levia would like that and wouldn't she be surprised? Maybe she'd even swoon.

In the book shop, he explained to the assistant, "It had some sort of bright cover. Pink maybe or yellow and there were shoes on it. Or a cake …maybe wine glasses?"

"It was a romance?"

"Yes!"

He was shown the romance section.

Sydney picked one up. "This might have been it. Or maybe that one… They're all pretty much the same, aren't they?"

The girl looked doubtful. "They have things in common, I suppose."

Sydney flicked through a few, looking for common themes.

1. Handsome, suntanned hero, showing off broad shoulders and perfect abs. Check. OK, he didn't have a tan, but he was still in pretty good shape. For his age. Considering.

2. Exotic cocktails. Check. Levia liked a drink in the evening after supper. He'd mix her up something special.

3. Browsing colourful stalls for unusual purchases. Check. It was market day.

Three should be enough. Any more might turn romance into full on passion and Sydney wasn't sure he had the strength for that.

At the market Sydney bought two aubergines, garlic and a bag of sprouts. He hadn't had sprouts for ages.

Levia didn't swoon. Sydney wasn't entirely sure what swooning looked like, but he was fairly sure her puzzled frown wasn't it. Luckily he had two more arrows in his cupid's bow of romantic gestures.

"Would you like a drink, love?" he asked after a slightly peculiar supper.

"Oh, yes please!"

It was working already! She sounded just as enthusiastic as she had the first time he'd offered her a drink all those years ago. She wouldn't fit in that mini skirt now, but his Levia was still a fine figure of a woman who deserved to be treated right.

Sydney poured half a glass of wine, added a generous measure of Ribena and topped it off with some of his beer. It didn't look as exotic as he'd hoped. What it really needed was one of those umbrella things and a cherry. A search of the kitchen cupboards revealed cocktail sticks and raisins. Sydney did the best he could, then unbuttoned his shirt in an enticing manner. The fake tan had worked much better on his clothes than his skin, but no matter.

He swaggered into the living room, presented the drink to Levia with a flourish and apologised for spilling some of it over her.

"Sydney, what's got into you?"

"Just being romantic."

She laughed so hard she spilled more than he had.

"It's not working is it?" He couldn't think where he'd gone wrong, but he must have done.

"No, but I appreciate you trying."

This romance lark was harder than a crossword, but he wasn't going to be beaten.

Sydney went back to the bookshop for further research. Sailing sounded dangerous, anything involving animals also had the potential to go badly wrong and one book was full of things which no amount of cod liver oil capsules could make him flexible enough for.

"Can I help at all?" the assistant asked. She didn't look hopeful.

"If you can tell me why women read these things."

"Because they like the escapism?"

Of course! That's what Levia had said. He'd listened and now he'd act. A bagful of books would bring romance into her life. But which had she already read? He explained the problem to the girl.

"You could get book tokens and let her choose."

That sounded more practical than romantic, so to help things along he bought a pretty pink card and more fake tan.

Levia looked just a tiny bit suspicious as she took the card from the envelope.

"This is for me?"

It was then he noticed the words 'congratulations on the birth of your twin girls' printed on the card.

"Er, yes. I liked the picture, but it's what's inside that counts."

"Very true," she said. She read where he'd written 'Love from Sydney x', then fanned out the book tokens.

Levia didn't speak, or move, or even blink. Was that swooning? He imagined it would be a bit more active than that.

"They're so you can buy those books you like."

"Sydney! Just when I thought you didn't understand me at

all!" She squeezed him round the middle and kissed the end of his nose.

"Are you swooning at me?"

"I am, Sidney. I am. Now take that shirt off."

"Eh?"

"Reckon I'm going to have to boil it."

"Right you are. Put the kettle on while you're at it will you, love?"

24. A Bag For Life

Erin stomped her way round the supermarket. Nothing was going right; her wrist hurt like crazy, the trolley only had three good wheels and she'd forgotten to bring a bag for life with her. Again. Those things were a bit like men Erin thought. A good idea in theory and sometimes a good idea in practice but often not where you wanted them to be.

Steve should be here helping. He'd offered in a half-hearted way yesterday. He hadn't offered again this morning before they'd both left for work; Steve driving the car, Erin catching the bus. She'd just have to fight through the pain of her sprained wrist and gather a few essentials for their breakfast tomorrow. She headed for the bread aisle.

"Blast!" she shrieked as the trolley took a lurch to the left, jamming itself into the shelving and painfully jolting her arm.

"Can I be of help?" asked an extremely attractive man.

Erin just gazed up into his deep blue eyes. How perfect. Just when she needed help, here was a man offering it. Not just any man, but one who was definitely tall enough to reach things from the top shelf.

"You look like you need a hand," the man said. He winked and pointed to the strapping on her wrist.

"Oh, er, yes. Could you pass me a brown sliced loaf, please?"

"My pleasure." His husky voice and smile suggested

pleasure was indeed something on his mind.

Once he'd got the loaf, he turned his attention to the trolley. To drag it free of the shelving he stood very close to Erin and curled one arm around her waist as he grabbed the trolley's handle. It wasn't until it was back in the centre of the aisle it occurred to her that she could easily have stepped away from him.

Her rescuer gave the sticky wheel a few sharp kicks. "I think that's freed it up a bit." He laid his hand on her shoulder. "Now, is there anything else I can do for you?"

Erin felt herself blush. "Um, no. Thanks." The wheel on her trolley might be free, but she wasn't.

She couldn't buy much shopping as one bag was all she could carry. Pity in a way because he really was the ideal man to help her with her shopping. She wondered what his name was. It wouldn't be anything plain like Steve. Something like Xavier would suit him. Her Steve was like a plastic carrier bag, except unlike a carrier bag he wouldn't be waiting at the checkout to help carry her groceries home. Xavier wasn't a carrier bag. If he was any kind of bag at all, it would be something expensive and stylish.

Erin wondered what was the ideal way to carry shopping. Maybe those trollies that elderly ladies sometimes used. You could get an awful lot in them, usually far more than elderly ladies seemed to buy. They'd be better for young mums with a family to feed. They'd be handy for leaning on if you got tired but what use where they when not shopping? They must be awkward to drag onto the bus and they'd be a pain at home taking up valuable storage space.

A rucksack would be good for small amounts but that'd mean shopping every day and Erin didn't want to do that. She had better things to do, such as snuggling up with her

Steve – even if he was a bit like an ordinary carrier bag.

Erin picked up a carton of milk and headed for the checkout. She considered buying one of the smart hessian shopping bags the supermarket had on offer. That might be a little easier to carry although she wasn't so sure about that as the handle looked rather small. It wouldn't be much use next time though as she was likely to forget to bring it with her and even if she did bring it, it'd be more awkward to carry folded in her handbag than the plastic ones were.

Maybe that was the kind of bag Xavier would be; attractive but impractical? As though her thoughts had conjured him up, he appeared next to her. He gave that gorgeous smile again, then helped her manoeuvre her trolley to the side of the checkout and reached for the little plastic triangle to put between her shopping and his. He winked at her again too. She didn't object to a good looking man winking at her, or trying to help her even if it was just an excuse to flirt, but she couldn't help noticing his own shopping now included flowers, condoms and champagne.

"Would you like a bag for life?" the checkout girl asked.

Erin didn't want one, nor cashback or someone to do her packing. If she wanted help she'd she'd ask, wouldn't she?

No, she probably wouldn't, just as she hadn't asked her husband to come and pick her up. When he'd offered she'd said there was no need. Or rather she'd snapped that she could cope. Then as the checkout girl had just reminded her, she'd forgotten her bag for life. Just as she'd almost forgotten her husband when Xavier smiled at her.

There was nothing wrong with an ordinary carrier bag she told herself as she paid for her groceries. It wasn't the most environmentally friendly option, but she could still re-use it (if she remembered) and it would do the job although not at all stylishly. At least she hoped it would do the job, the handles didn't feel all that secure as she lifted it off the till. Not at all like her Steve then. He was reliable. If he said he'd do something he did it. She was as sure as she could be that if he were out buying flowers for her he wouldn't be winking at other pretty girls before he paid for them.

"Would you like a bag for life?" Erin heard the cashier ask Xavier.

"Yes, I'd like a new one in exchange for this one, please."

Erin glanced back to see him hand over a bag that was looking a little tatty but still seemed perfectly serviceable. Her Steve wouldn't do that to her either, she was sure. He liked how she looked, but he hadn't married her just for her shiny hair and neat figure.

"There you are, love," said a large cardboard box on which was balanced a bunch of brightly coloured flowers. "I was worried I'd taken too long and would miss you."

It wasn't a box at all, it was Steve. Well, there was a box of shopping, but Steve carried it and it was he who'd spoken.

"I know you didn't want to make a fuss about your wrist but I was worried about you trying to carry anything with it so I decided to do the shopping myself. I was hoping to catch you before you started."

"Don't worry, I just got some milk, apples and bread."

"Oh good. Chuck them in here then and I'll carry them."

Xavier passed them as Erin added her shopping to the items in Steve's cardboard box, but she didn't glance up to see if he seemed disappointed she was no longer alone. Erin linked her good arm with the one Steve was using to steady the box and walked with him towards the car park. He really had found the perfect way to carry their shopping.

25. Love Will Wait

Jennie met Kieran during her first week of secondary school. He proposed on their last day. It never occurred to sixteen-year-old Jennie to say no. They were blissfully in love and had so much in common. They'd been friends for five years, dating for two. Her family liked him, his liked her. Kieran even had a fairy godmother, called Aunt Flo, who'd given them her blessing. Marrying him would ensure Jennie lived happily ever after.

Her school friends and Kieran's sister would make beautiful bridesmaids and Jennie would have a fantastic white dress with a veil and long train in matching lace. They'd fill the church with family and flowers. Chocolate, she thought for the wedding cake. Dark and rich in the centre with a white chocolate coating for a traditional look. Or maybe a tower of individual cup cakes in various shades of pink, each topped with a sugar heart. Children would throw rose petals as confetti and Aunt Flo would sprinkle them with a glittery shower of fairy dust.

They'd go somewhere sunny on honeymoon, then set up a home together. It wouldn't be a big place, but they'd paint it in cheery colours and she'd borrow Mum's sewing machine to make pretty curtains and heaps of cushions, for the sofa and bed, in gorgeous fabrics. They'd have flowers and scented candles in every room and cook dinner together each night.

It wasn't until she showed her parents the ring that her

fairytale life hit its first big hurdle. Mum and Dad didn't welcome Kieran into the family as a future son.

Instead, Dad said, "I thought you two had more sense! Kieran, I think you'd better go."

"What do you mean 'no'?" Jennie asked once she'd got over the shock enough to speak. "It's my life, my decision."

"You can't get married at sixteen. You're a child still," Dad said.

"Try to be a bit practical," Mum said.

Not practical? She'd thought it all through.

Mum continued to point out obstacles, mainly financial as though money mattered when you were in love! She ended with, "And what about your A levels?"

All right, they were young and there weren't likely to be many other married students in the sixth form college, but Jennie didn't see why that mattered.

"My parents said the same as yours," Kieran told her the next day.

Eventually they were persuaded to wait until they were eighteen at least. They refused the suggestion to consider dating other people and Jennie continued to wear Kieran's ring.

"My fairy godmother said not to worry. Love will wait," he told her one day.

His great aunt Flo really did look just like a Disney fairy. Not the slender, Tinkerbell type, but the little, round 'get Cinderella to the ball' type. She also had something of a reputation as a matchmaker and solver of problems. With her on side, everything would work out.

Jennie and Kieran both worked extremely hard, partly to prove to their families that continuing the relationship was not a mistake. As a result they both got good grades and were accepted by their first choice of university. By then, Jennie felt sure her parents had been right. She still loved Kieran as much as ever, but marriage and schoolwork wouldn't have gone together and where would they have lived? They did need to be practical.

"Let's take a gap year, see a bit of the world," Kieran said.

"We can't afford that and if we could it would be better to save the money so we can get married when we've finished university," Jennie said. Her parents had stressed the need to get on the property ladder at the earliest opportunity. For that they'd need jobs.

"So we're not getting married now?"

"I think it would be better to wait, Kieran. We'll still be together."

"If that's really what you want."

A friend of Jennie's dad had a staff vacancy. She wouldn't get her degree, but she could do day release for a qualification in the same area and the experience would be valuable. They'd be better off in the short term and probably no worse off in the long run.

Kieran wasn't sure. "It's not what you'd planned."

"No, but it is practical and …maybe we could live together?"

Eagerly he sat with her and tried to calculate if it was possible for them to buy a home together. They worked out it almost was, if that home was tiny and in an unpopular area and they were accepted for a mortgage with the lowest possible monthly repayments. For that to happen Jennie's potential employer must allow her to work from the northernmost of the company's offices, Kieran would have to switch to a less prestigious university and take a part time job, and someone would have to give them a deposit.

After all Dad's talk about the importance of owning a home Jennie hadn't expected it to be such a challenge to persuade him to advance them the money he'd put aside for her wedding. When Mum saw the bleak flat over a boarded up shop the struggle became even harder.

"We've waited, just like you asked us to and isn't buying a flat a more practical idea than spending a fortune on a wedding and then in rent?" Jennie said.

"I see your point," Dad admitted.

Kieran had switched on his charm, painting a rosy image of the surrounding area and the projected rise in the value of their investment. His master stroke was taking them to tea with Aunt Flo who lived close by. Her flat was the same size as the one Jennie and Kieran hoped to buy, but cozily furnished and prettily decorated in pastel shades and floral prints. She used the type of china and served the kinds of cake you'd expect from a fairy godmother.

Afterwards they all went for a walk which somehow took them past an estate agency. Aunt Flo walked slowly enough for Dad to notice the price of property in the better end of town.

She pointed out the half completed industrial estate. "By the time Kieran finishes university, there will be lots of job opportunities," she said.

Later she offered to give them their wedding present early and try to persuade Kieran's parents to do the same, if it would help. Aunt Flo's gift wasn't a large sum, only enough to have bought them a really good vacuum cleaner but, when added to what both their parents contributed, it was just enough to make the difference.

Jennie and Kieran were ecstatic when their offer was accepted. Getting everything sorted out meant they didn't have a break between leaving college and starting work and university, but they were together, that's all that mattered.

They did their best to make the flat nice, painting it with leftover paint Kieran's dad had in his garage. Jennie adjusted charity shop curtains and they gratefully accepted whatever secondhand linen their families could spare. There were no flowers, but at least the bloom of damp on the kitchen ceiling didn't spread. Their investment was safe and they had each other. Cosy nights in making plans didn't cost anything and they had fun keeping warm in ways which didn't involve putting the heating on.

Aunt Flo visited regularly. She was great at spotting grocery bargains, knowing who had secondhand furniture they'd be happy to have taken away, and cutting money off coupons from magazines. She also invited them round for a roast lunch quite often. Somehow her offer always coincided with times money was extra tight.

In addition to his university studies, Kieran worked three nights a week in term time stacking supermarket shelves. In the holidays he doubled that. Jennie worked four days a week all year round. She only attended college on Tuesdays but had as much coursework to do as she'd completed for her A levels. They still loved each other but, as the months went on, had little time or energy to show it. Tiredness led to occasional silly arguments.

"Look what was in the reduced section tonight," Kieran said once, producing a piece of fillet steak. "Only three pounds and I even got half price mushrooms to go with it."

"We could have bought enough tins of beans to last all week for that much!"

"I'm sick of baked beans," Kieran yelled. He'd slammed the fridge door so hard Jennie's mug, which had been precariously balanced on her work, fell and broke. Then he added, far more gently, "I thought we deserved a bit of a treat for our anniversary."

How could she have forgotten that he'd proposed exactly three years ago?

They made it up, just as they did the row over 'wasting' train fares to visit their parents.

"They come up quite often," Jennie pointed out.

"Yes, but not for Christmas. I know how much you missed your family last year and to be honest I'd like to see mine too," Kieran said.

"We've got Aunt Flo."

"True," he'd said, hugging her.

Despite moving away and having very different lifestyles, they retained some contact with former friends through social media. They read comments about drinking until three in the morning, saw photos taken during muddy musical festivals.

"I expect they're enjoying themselves, but it's not my idea of fun," Kieran said.

"Nor mine. We made the right choice for us, didn't we?"

Jennie was pleased with how practical she'd become. Drinking plain water not only saved the cost of milk and teabags, but on electricity too. At least it would if Kieran could remember to measure how much water he needed and not boil half a kettle full each time.

She requested something useful for every birthday and Christmas present. Everyone but Aunt Flo went along with her wishes.

"It's probably all she can afford," Kieran pointed out when Jennie had been disappointed to receive a beautifully wrapped box of chocolates.

Tea towels wouldn't have been any more expensive, but it was kind of Aunt Flo to give her anything and it was lovely to cuddle up with Kieran and enjoy some luxury for a change. It reminded them their current struggles were temporary and they'd soon both have much better jobs, a flat which had increased in value and a wonderful life together ahead of them.

Every now and then Jennie nagged him about his minor extravagances or Kieran complained about her penny pinching, but usually they compromised. He liked her hair longer and thought she was just as pretty without make-up. She was happy to save on salon fees and the cost of lipstick.

Jennie hadn't budgeted for buying a microwave, even one Kieran bought very cheaply from work as it was scratched, but it was very convenient and would earn its keep by saving gas.

Their big row came when Kieran was promoted to a supervisory role in the supermarket. He still worked nights and still stacked shelves for most of the time, but he had a little more responsibility and a tiny rise in pay.

"We should increase our mortgage payments," Jennie said.

"No! This is going towards something more important."

"More important than the mortgage?"

"What about all our plans, Jennie? The wedding? Travel?"

"We have to be practical."

"Practical yes, obsessed no."

Jennie wasn't obsessed. It wasn't that she didn't want to marry Kieran, she did so much, but weddings were expensive. Even the cheapest wedding dress cost more than she'd allowed herself for clothes since she'd left school. The smallest cake was more expensive than they spent on food in a fortnight and there would have to be a reception. There was no way they could repay another loan. Their families had already given them all they could when they'd bought the flat. She'd accepted the fairytale wedding she'd once dreamed off just wouldn't happen, why couldn't Kieran make a few sacrifices too?

She did try to calmly explain all that, but somehow ended up yelling that he was putting a holiday ahead of their future together.

"Jennie, we need to start living. I want a future that's more," he gestured round the flat. "More than this."

"I thought I was your future," she said, but by then he'd already left for work.

She hardly slept that night. When she did, it was to dream of Aunt Flo waving a wand and creating flowers, cakes and a wonderful lace dress. As Jennie floated up the aisle, sunlight streaming through the stained glass windows turned dust motes into sparkles of colour. Kieran, in an immaculate morning suit, waited for her at the altar.

In the morning she had grit in her eye, Kieran was still in his supermarket uniform and she saw he'd bought more food they didn't need.

"I'd rather have marmalade on my toast now, than pay off the mortgage when I'm fifty-nine and eleven months instead of sixty," he told her.

She snatched up the jar.

"Hey, don't throw that at me. It'd be a waste of thirty-seven pence."

Jennie saw the reduced label and burst into tears.

"Hey, come on, love. It's going to be OK." He reached out for her. "We've got a fairy godmother, remember?"

Jennie pushed him away. "Unless she dies and we're in her will what good does that do us?"

"Jennie! What's happened to you? Is money all you care about?"

"No of course not!" Why would he think that?

Then she realised what she'd said. How could she have been so horrible? Aunt Flo had been fantastic. Her finances weren't much better than theirs, but she'd greatly enriched their lives. On nice days she'd dragged them out for walks. She found out about free events they might be interested in and urged them to attend. The thrifty recipes she'd taught them provided tasty meals and they'd had fun playing her old board games.

"Kieran, I didn't mean that. Really I didn't."

"I didn't think so." He held her close and gently rubbed her back until she stopped crying, then wiped away her tears and kissed her.

"And did you mean it, about spending your pay rise?" she asked.

"Not spending, saving for something important."

"I'd love a holiday too, Kieran and you do deserve one, but …"

"It's not important? That's true, love, but our wedding is don't you think?"

"We can't afford it."

"That's what I told Aunt Flo. Sit down and I'll give you her answer."

Kieran fetched an envelope and a pen. "Write down on there the really important things about getting married."

Jennie took the pen and frowned. Whatever they might call Aunt Flo and however much his godmother might want to help them, she couldn't wave a wand and make their wishes come true.

"Come on, love. You're good at making practical lists."

He looked so hopeful, Jennie knew she must try. A fabulous dress came to mind. She'd still like that, but it wasn't important. Obviously she couldn't be naked, but she did have some clothes, or perhaps she could borrow something a bit glamorous. Of course she would like a huge cake and to provide a nice meal for family and friends, but all those who really cared about them would be there even if there was nothing. They'd been living together for two years and had their own home so a honeymoon wasn't exactly vital.

'Kieran' was all she wrote.

"Here's mine," he said and handed her a crumpled piece of paper with 'Jennie' written on it. "I was going to show you straight away and try to talk you round, but that night I was asked if I'd like to apply to be supervisor at the supermarket and decided to wait. I knew if I got it, we could afford a few non essentials. A cake, flowers …"

"Kieran, that would be wonderful."

"Really?"

"Yes, really. It'll be a very practical dream come true."

"If we did a lot of it ourselves, maybe we could manage some kind of reception?"

"Remember the teeny pumpkin shaped pies, shortbread crowns and cheese straws which looked like castle turrets that Aunt Flo had us making at Christmas? I bet she's got plenty more budget buffet recipes."

"Bound to have and I had an idea about the invitations." He showed her the enchanting sketch he'd made.

"That's lovely! My boss might let me print them at work."

"And I know mine will give us a good discount on food and drink."

They talked for hours about decorating the tables with sugar mice and rosy red apples, a cake made from gingerbread and Jennie's hair in a long, long plait. Of making 'drink me' and 'love potion' labels for the water jugs. How if they couldn't find smart clothes they'd wear rags as Cinderella and Buttons. About which uncle was a good photographer and which had a nice car he might drive Jennie to the church in.

"I need a cup of tea," Kieran said. "Do you want one, or water?"

"Tea please. There's one chocolate left, want to share?"

As he made the drinks, Jennie put together the two mini lists with just their names written on. "I'm starting the guest list." As she wrote 'Aunt Flo' she noticed the tatty old envelopes were both covered with a sprinkling of glitter as fine as dust. How could that have got there?

Thank you for reading this book. I hope you enjoyed it. If you did, I'd really appreciate it if you could leave a short review on Amazon and/or Goodreads.

To learn more about my writing life, hear about new releases and get a free exclusive ebook, sign up to my newsletter – subscribepage.io/ItLSNa or you can find the link on my website patsycollins.co.uk

More books by Patsy Collins

Novels

Firestarter

Escape To The Country

A Year And A Day

Paint Me A Picture

Leave Nothing But Footprints

Acting Like A Killer

Little Mallow cosy mystery series

Disguised Murder and Community Spirit in Little Mallow

Dependable Friends and Deceitful Neighbours
in Little Mallow

Deadly Words and Innocent Gossip in Little Mallow

Short story collections

Over The Garden Fence
Up The Garden Path
Through The Garden Gate
In The Garden Air
Beyond The Garden Wall

No Family Secrets
Can't Choose Your Family
Keep It In The Family
Family Feeling
Happy Families

All That Love Stuff
With Love And Kisses
Love Is The Answer

Slightly Spooky Stories I
Slightly Spooky Stories II
Slightly Spooky Stories III
Slightly Spooky Stories IV
Slightly Spooky Stories V

Just A Job
Perfect Timing
A Way With Words
Dressed To Impress
Coffee & Cake
Not A Drop To Drink